WINTER KING

THE WYTH COURTS BOOK 1

JULIANA HAYGERT

COPYRIGHT

WINTER KING

His court is dying, and she's his only hope ...

Monsters of the Tywyll Forest have poisoned the Winter Court, unleashing a prophecy that demands a human sacrifice to save the withering land. Willing to do whatever it takes to save his people, King Cadewyn of the Winter Court ventures to the human world in search of one insignificant life to claim...

Amber was used to her life being in shambles, but getting kidnapped and whisked off to a magical fae realm was a new low, even for her. While feeling drawn to the fae King by a sizzling attraction, her apprehension builds to a panic over why he brought her there.

When Cade discovers that Amber is his mate, can he still carry out his plan to sacrifice her? Or will the malicious plotting of others within the court leave Amber trapped in the mystical realm with nowhere to run?

Winter King is a standalone steamy paranormal romance with a HEA. Each book in the Wyth Courts series will feature a different couple, with a complete story, and a HEA. Suited for readers 18+ due to language and sex scenes.

AUTHOR'S NOTE

I HOPE you enjoy reading *Winter King*!

IF YOU WANT to know about new releases, upcoming books, giveaways, and more, don't forget to sign up for my Newsletter!

Want to see exclusive teasers, help me decide on covers, read excerpts, talk about books, etc? Then join my reader group on Facebook: Juliana's Club!

1

CADE

THE REPORT I got this morning was nothing like I expected.

"Have you seen this?" I asked Kei, my most trusted general, as I reread the words scribbled on the paper.

They couldn't be right.

"I have, Cade," Kei said, his voice strained. "It's even worse than they described. I think you should come with me and see it for yourself."

"Snow above," I muttered under my breath as I rolled the paper back up and dropped it on the long table in my study alongside many other reports and scriptures. I had so much to do, but this...if this was true, it couldn't wait. I gestured to Kei. "Lead the way."

Kei's long body shimmered and changed. His white and silver armor disappeared, giving way to light gray fur as he hunkered down and shook his tail behind him. As a wolf, he let out a short yelp, letting me know he was ready.

I changed too, but as the king of the Winter Court, my wolf was pure white and much bigger than Kei's.

I'm ready, I told him through the link we shared when in our wolf forms.

Without another second to waste, Kei dashed away, and I followed. We ran through the hallways and down the stairs of the White Palace, dodging servants and guards who were going about their days.

The moment I stepped out of the palace, the six White Knights, who had been standing there and waiting, shifted into their wolf forms and followed us. Kei was the general of my army, but the White Knights were my personal bodyguards. I liked to think I didn't need them, so I kept them outside the palace. But since we didn't know much about the threat mentioned in this morning's report, I had them come with us.

The eight of us ran out of the palace grounds, through the White City, and into the forest, where we could stretch our legs and use our full speed. We zoomed through the snow, past leafless trees and broken branches.

What would take eight hours by horse took us two hours in our wolf forms.

We're almost there, Kei said into our minds.

He slowed down, and we followed suit. The trees gave way to a valley, where one of the border towers was located, but instead of being covered in snow, the ground was pitch-black.

I shifted into my fae form. "What in the frost is this?"

The guards who usually stayed at the tower appeared before me.

"It started overnight, my king," Aimon said, his head low. "It's unlike anything I've ever seen. It started right at the border, and like a wave, it has been spreading over the land."

"It took over the tower," Birch said, pointing to the once-white tower, now a mass of dark gray crumbles. "We tried to fight it with our powers, to push it back, but it didn't budge. Whatever this is, we can't stop it."

As we watched, the darkness spread some more. It was slow, but every five minutes or so, it advanced half an inch, melting the snow and killing the land underneath, turning everything black.

My brow furrowed. What could this be? With steady steps, I advanced toward it.

"My king, be careful," Kei said, using formal speech. He only called me by my name when we were alone.

I heard him, but I had to know what in the frost was this. I crouched down, stretched my arm, and slid my index and middle fingers from the snow to the darkness.

The moment the darkness touched my skin, it burned worse than the Summer Court's sun.

"Snow above," I hissed, pulling back.

Kei and the six White Knights were all over me in a flash, but I pushed them away. Staring at the advancing darkness, I took several steps back. I didn't care about the pain in my fingertips. That would pass, and with the magic in my veins, I would soon heal.

But what about my land?

I glanced around. "Who did this?" From here, all I could see was the valley in front of us, now black because of the darkness, and beyond the dried Triad River and the Tywyll Forest.

A land of monsters.

"We don't know, my king," Aimon said. "But we have reason to believe it was the Tabred."

A wave of rage coursed through me, and I suppressed a growl. The Tywyll Forest was a land without a ruler, but that only meant many groups existed and fought against each other and against the Wyth courts. One of these groups, the Tabred, had been at war with my court for centuries.

After I killed their leader years ago, the group had been oddly quiet.

Until now.

This freezing thing happened. I inhaled deeply and channeled my magic. It filled my veins. Ice, snow, frost, wind—it was all part of me, part of my court. It was who I was, what I lived and breathed for.

"Stand back," I rasped.

Kei, the White Knights, and the border guards took many steps back.

And I let out my magic. It blew like an avalanche, relentless in its path. If a lesser fae had stood there, it would have been obliterated in less than a second. A higher fae would be able to withstand it for a minute or two, but it would weaken him and eventually kill him.

The Winter Court was me, and I was the Winter Court. There was nothing stronger, faster, more powerful than me, not in this land. Not in my kingdom. And anyone who threatened my people, my court, would suffer the consequences.

I sent all my magic, all its vast power, to the darkness, sure I could revert it. Sure I could make it disappear.

But minutes later when I pulled back, breathing hard from the effort, I was dumbfounded to find the darkness hadn't moved back one inch. In fact, it only advanced a little more.

"What in the frost?" I had no words, no idea, no action.

Nothing had ever resisted the full power of my magic before.

"What should we do, my king?" Kei asked, his tone guarded, as if afraid of my answer.

I opened my mouth, but no freezing word came out, because I didn't know.

"It's a curse," a new voice said.

I turned and saw her.

Mahaera, the kind and gentle goddess of Wyth. Her long, white hair moved behind her as if she were underwater, and her long, white dress hugged her voluptuous form.

"A curse?" I asked her. If someone could tell me what this was and how to fix it, it was one of the three sister goddesses.

Mahaera offered me a tight smile, but her dark eyes remained serene. "The Tabred has put a curse on your land."

"This is…." I pressed my lips tight. Unacceptable? Insane? Many colorful words flew through my mind.

"Tell us what to do, my king," Kei said, bowing his head low. "If you want me to gather our forces and attack them full force, I'll do so."

Mahaera tsked, her dark eyes fixed on the dying land. "Reigniting the war, which has been dormant for years, won't break this curse."

"What will?" I asked, taking a couple of steps toward her. "What will break this curse?"

She turned, fixing those wise eyes on mine. This version of her was calm and gentle, but she still always said the truth and impacted our lives more than we expected it in any of her versions. "Here's what you need to do…."

2

AMBER

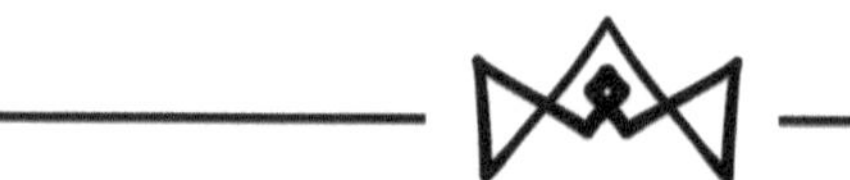

"I'm sorry, Amber, but there's no other way. I need to fire you."

I stared at Howard, not believing what I was hearing. "But...why?" I croaked. I knew I hadn't been employee of the year, but I was sure I didn't suck either.

"It's not just you," my boss said. *Or should I call him my ex-boss?* "Early this morning, I let Sabrina go, and tonight I'll have to do the same with Rick." He gestured around the main seating area of the restaurant. "It's lunch time and there's no one here. From what the owner told me, he'll have to fire half of the staff."

"Shit," I muttered.

The small, local Italian restaurant was never a big hit, but in the past few months, things had dwindled fast. For some reason, people just didn't come here anymore, and I felt bad for the owner. I also felt bad for Rick. He was almost seventy years old. He had been working here for over twenty years. After this gig, I doubted he would find something else.

As much as I hated being fired, I was one of the youngest here. I was also healthy and optimistic—at least on most days. I was sure I would find something soon to pay my bills.

I unknotted the apron from around my waist and handed it to Howard.

"I'm so sorry," he said, his tone upset.

"It's okay." I tried smiling, but at that moment, I wasn't feeling much like it.

"Take this." Howard grabbed a brown bag from the table beside us. "It's your favorite, chicken parmigiana. I thought you should have a treat before leaving like this."

I took the bag from him, and this time my small smile was genuine. "Thank you."

"It's the least I could do." Howard rocked on the balls of his feet. "Take care, Amber."

"You too," I whispered.

This was it. Another page of my life turned. Another phase that had come to an end and would hopefully lead to a new beginning. Seeing as I was only twenty-one and had had so many new beginnings, I was starting to think things weren't going so well for me.

With the brown bag in hand, I exited the restaurant.

And the façade crumbled.

I was optimistic most of the time, yes, but right now I felt like a lost puppy shuffling down the street with his tail between his legs.

My life had never been easy. My father had been a quiet man with barely any emotions. When my mother died when I was fourteen, he shut down completely. It was like living with a stranger.

Then a couple of years later, out of the blue, he introduced me to a new woman—a total witch. She hated me almost as much as I hated her. She convinced him to move away and start over, but without me. So at seventeen, I was abandoned. At first, I tried moving on, staying in my hometown, but neighbors became nosy, people whispered behind my back, and social services came after me, wanting to put me in the system. I did my best to dodge them, but once my eighteenth birthday came around, I left too.

I left, and I never looked back.

I settled in Brooksville, this tiny town in the middle of nowhere. Though some people were a little wary of me at first—I mean, what eighteen-year-old girl showed up in a small town by herself?—most treated me well.

That had been three years ago.

With a sigh, I crossed the street and went about my business. I wouldn't go down memory lane, and I wouldn't go down a sad path. I would remain optimistic through all of this journey. I had to.

Otherwise I would break down.

I inhaled the chilly air, welcoming the clarity it brought to my head. It was mid-November, and the temperatures were dropping fast. I didn't really like winter; that was why I had moved from New Hampshire to Georgia. It still got cold here, but not as much as the north.

Half a block later, I walked by a narrow alley between two shops. Movement caught my eye. I halted and saw an old man rummaging through the trash cans, a piece of orange peel in his hand. The man turned his eyes to me, and his ghastly face sent a pang through my chest. It wasn't just the face. It was everything. His clothes were in tatters, he probably hadn't had a shower in weeks, and his legs were almost as thin as my arms. The man was cold and starving.

Without hesitating, I approached him. "Here." I showed him the brown bag I had received at the restaurant. "You'll like it." The man's eyes became huge saucers. "Take it." I pushed the bag toward him.

His hands shook as he took the bag from me. "Thank you," he said, his voice frail, just like the rest of him.

The food wasn't enough, not for me, so I took off my jacket. It was a thin suede jacket that barely did anything. I would feel a little cold without it, but I would survive. "Take this too." I pushed the jacket to him.

"No, I can't take that," the old man said, his eyes huge again.

"I insist." I pushed the jacket toward him again.

He hesitated but grabbed the jacket. "Thank you, miss. God bless you."

I offered him a smile, then walked out of the alley so he could put on the jacket and eat in peace.

Perhaps I had just had a huge blow on my day, but it always warmed my heart when I could help out others. That meant that all was not lost yet.

With renewed determination, I ignored the cold and trudged to my favorite coffee shop. I usually ordered a latte and one of their famous croissants, but since I had to mind my budget even more now, I asked for a black coffee.

With the coffee in hand—aka, my lunch—I took a seat at a table by the large glass windows, pulled my long black hair in a messy bun, and started playing with my phone. Instead of browsing through Facebook and Instagram, I went directly to job hunting websites and searched for local gigs.

That was the disadvantage of living in a small town: there weren't many opportunities around. I saw a few things that would require I worked overtime with a measly salary. I also saw lots of manual jobs that required strength and agility. At five foot four, and with my small frame that could be carried by the wind, I wouldn't survive a day.

I let out a long sigh and looked out the window. It was the middle of my first day without a job. I couldn't lose hope just yet.

***

DESPITE TRYING to avoid my apartment, I couldn't wander around town all day long, especially not without a jacket. Besides, I was tired and emotionally exhausted. I had to go home, take a nice, long shower, and sleep. Tomorrow, after a good rest, I would regroup my thoughts and start a new search.

Praying Kimberly wasn't home, I opened the door and stepped in.

"What the hell are you doing here at this hour?"

I inhaled deeply and tried to not let the image in front of me bother me too much. Kimberly stood in the middle of our tiny living room, wearing only a bra and panties, with a lit cigarette in one hand and nail clippers in the other. There were two empty beer bottles on the coffee table in front of her, just beside all her dead nails.

Her fake blonde hair was pulled into several foam rollers, and her makeup could be seen from three miles away.

I closed the door behind me. "What did we say about smoking inside the apartment?"

She shrugged and took another long puff. "I wasn't expecting you so early."

I glanced at the minuscule black dress over our torn couch. "And I see you're going somewhere early."

"It's just a party," she said with a smile. Kimberly was all about parties, all freaking day long. "A small thing at the Dark Rose Pub."

It was always a small thing. So small, she would crawl back home with barely any clothes left and not remembering one single thing, other than she had screwed someone. Who? Only Heaven knew.

"Have f—"

"You should come," she said, surprising me. Other than the necessary topics of two roommates, like bills and grocery shopping, we didn't talk much. We had tried in the beginning, but after a couple of days living together, it was clear we had nothing in common. "Maybe you can loosen up a little and let someone finally get between your legs."

There it was. The reason for this entire conversation. She wanted, once more, to throw in my face that I was a virgin. It had been my mistake, really. When I first moved in with her, I tried being friends and telling her a little about me. Like a stupid innocent girl at eighteen, I told her I had never had sex. After that, she used every occasion she had to tease me about it.

Unfortunately, the situation hadn't changed in the last three years. I hadn't met anyone who interested me enough to move on from first base within this little town, and she knew that.

Unlike her, I wouldn't go out to get stupidly drunk and sleep with just anyone. It wasn't me. Actually, just thinking about it made my stomach knot. Maybe it was silly of me, but I still believed the man who would sweep me off my feet was out there and one day I would find him.

And we would live happily ever after.

Kimberly let out a boisterous laugh, as if she had just told the joke of the year.

I rolled my eyes and went to my bedroom. I closed the door and rested my back against the thin wood. Living here with her was killing my spirit, but this was the cheapest place I could find in Brooksville, and now I wasn't even sure I would be able to continue paying for it.

My eyes filled with tears, but I pushed them away. It was still too early for that. I had just been fired. I couldn't fall into despair just yet.

Tomorrow would be a new day, a better day. I knew it.

I willed it so.

My dreams were riddled with the most horrible thing on Earth: a huge credit card bill I couldn't pay.

I tossed and turned, desperately trying to rest, so I really could make my day better tomorrow, but my mind wouldn't shut down. I stayed in bed, though, counting little sheep, hoping sleep would come take me.

Instead, my phone rang at four in the morning.

"What the...?" I reached for it, and the caller's name flashed on the screen: Dark Rose Pub. I exhaled through my nose as irritation filled my veins. "Hello?"

"Hey, Amber, it's me, Judd," the owner of the pub said.

"Let me guess, Kimberly is passed out in a corner and you want me to come pick her up."

"As usual," he muttered.

Every time I went there to collect Kimberly, which was at least twice a month, the old man looked at me with pure pity. I hated that, but I never said anything. Even though I also hated the fact that Kimberly drank herself to oblivion and put me in this position, I couldn't just leave her there. What if some bad guy tried to abuse her? I didn't want that on my conscience.

So I sat up in bed and sighed. "I'll be right there."

3

CADE

I HADN'T EXPECTED movement in the middle of the night, but sure enough, the female human left her apartment building in a hurry just after four in the morning. She hugged a thin jacket over a tee and sweatpants. A second later, a taxi showed up and she boarded it.

Where in the freezing ice was she going at this time?

Regardless of my thoughts, I changed into my wolf form and followed her.

Just like I had done all day long.

Right after Mahaera told me how to save my people, I used my medallion to teleport to the human world. Mahaera had helped. She cast a spell over me, saying I would end up near the one I needed to save my court.

A selfless, pure-hearted human.

When she told me that, I scoffed. A selfless, pure-hearted human? Those were myths. They didn't exist. But Mahaera assured me I just had to get near the human and I would know.

The moment I saw Amber leaving the restaurant after being fired, with her long, black hair whipping in the chilly wind and her bright green eyes looking up at the clear skies full of hope and wonder, I knew it was her. Not because she was absolutely stunning and I couldn't take my eyes off her, but because the pull I felt deep in my core told me that she was the one I needed.

She was the only one who could save my people.

That idea only got stronger when I saw her stopping by a homeless man and giving her jacket and lunch to him. Then she'd walked around town in a thin sweater and later had just a coffee, as if that was enough to keep her healthy.

If that wasn't selfless, then I didn't know what was.

The taxi stopped in front of a pub. Amber got out of the car. "Wait here, please," she said to the driver before running inside.

I shifted back into my fae form and clenched my fists. I had been to the human world a few times before, and I knew what happened inside these places. It wasn't much different from the taverns in my fae realm, but I still didn't like seeing Amber walking in there alone in the middle of the night.

I told myself it was just a natural protective feeling. What if something bad happened to her before she could save my land? I couldn't allow that to happen.

So I started toward the pub, but she stepped out a moment later with another female draped around her shoulders, clearly too drunk to stand on her own.

"Come on, Kimberly," she hissed between gritted teeth. Kimberly was taller than her, making it difficult for Amber to carry her. "Help me here, please."

But Kimberly didn't hear her, or she didn't care. Amber

continued bearing most of her friend's weight, shuffling toward the taxi. Snow above, couldn't the driver step out and help? What kind of manners were humans taught?

I started moving again when three men stepped out of the pub and surrounded Amber and her friend.

"Hey, pretty little thing," one of them drawled. "How about you bring your friend and we go play?"

Amber's arms tightened around Kimberly. "We're fine."

"Come on," another one said, his voice even more slurred than the first guy. He tripped over his own feet as he reached for Amber. "It'll be fun."

Amber took a step back, almost falling down with Kimberly's dead weight.

The third guy was right there, at her back, and he closed his hands around her shoulders. "We'll show you a good time, pretty girl."

Something vile, something powerful coursed through me. I wanted to ram into those men and shred them to pieces with my claws and teeth, but I didn't want to scare Amber more than she already was.

Going for another tactic, I stopped just out of sight and channeled my magic. I sent ice to envelop those men's legs and arms, so they couldn't move, so they couldn't touch Amber without her permission.

The moment she realized she had an opening, Amber jolted forward, dragging her friend with her, and slid inside the taxi as fast as she could.

The taxi drove away while the men shouted at them.

"You frigid little bitch!" one of them hollered.

Like a predator, I stepped out of my hiding spot and stalked to the men.

"Having fun?" I asked.

The three men sneered at me. "Mind your own business," one of them spat.

Well, Amber was my business.

I called on my magic, and more ice and frost rose, covering every inch of the men's bodies. My will was to kill them, or to at least punch them until their teeth fell out, but I couldn't risk it. The human world was too different than mine, and I had to *try* not to cause any problems here.

The men whimpered, trying to move and speak, but with my ice all over them, all they could do was bug out their eyes and make some sounds.

"Stay away from innocent women," I told them through gritted teeth.

Then I walked away.

In about fifteen minutes, when they were close to hypothermia, the ice would melt away. The men would probably need to go to an ER, but after what they did, they deserved it.

I continued down the street with long, sure steps, though I wasn't feeling so sure anymore. This was supposed to be a simple task: come to Earth, find the one with the pure heart, take her back to Wyth.

That was all I was supposed to do, and yet, here I was, walking back to Amber's apartment to make sure she had gotten there all right.

"Snow above," I cursed, tugging at my pants. These human clothes were too thick and tight. How was one supposed to walk and simply move in tight jeans and a fitted shirt?

Relief washed through me once I arrived at her building

and saw the light of her apartment window come on. She walked in front of the window before closing the curtains.

She was safe.

For now.

From me.

But time was running out.

4

AMBER

LAST NIGHT WAS one of the shittiest of my entire life. First, I couldn't sleep because I had been fired. Then I was called to pick up Kimberly—again. She was barely conscious, which made getting her to the cab nearly impossible. Then three men harassed us just outside the pub, and to complete the night, Kimberly threw up all over my legs and the carpet in our living room. After changing her and putting her to bed, I had to clean up our horrible carpet and take a shower myself.

It was almost six in the morning when I finally laid my head down on my pillow again.

And I got up thirty minutes later. I couldn't even blame my alarm clock this time, since I had remembered to turn it off last night. It was all due to habit. I used to get up, shower, and go to the restaurant, where there was tons to do before brunch.

Or there had been before it slowly started dying down.

Since I didn't have anything to do, I tried staying in bed and sleeping some more, but habit was a nasty thing.

So I threw my covers off and got up.

When I made my way to the kitchen to grab some coffee, Kimberly staggered out of her bedroom.

"What happened last night?" she asked, her eyes narrowed as if it hurt to open them. "Why am I here?"

Meaning, she should be in someone else's bed right now. I always tried to see the best in everyone, even when they were oh so screwed, but sometimes I had a hard time seeing anything good in Kimberly.

"Judd called saying you were wasted and alone again," I told her.

Her eyes widened. "And you went to pick me up? Why the hell?"

I blinked. Was she serious? She wanted me to leave her there? She didn't even remember me picking her up. Anyone could have taken her and done whatever with her, and she would never know. I wasn't asking for much in return, just a thank you would suffice.

"You know what? Forget it," she said, venom lacing her words. "I can't deal with you right now." She went back into her bedroom and slammed the door between us.

Holy shit. Well, I couldn't deal with her right now either.

Instead of having breakfast in the kitchen, I brewed some coffee and took it to my bedroom. I looked through my phone, searching for jobs again, but nothing had changed from yesterday.

And I was sure nothing would change tomorrow either.

I sat down at the edge of my bed, feeling sorry for myself.

No. No, I couldn't. Not yet. It was too soon.

With a renewed sense of purpose, I got up from my bed and got dressed.

I knew what I could do.

After four laps on the walking trails around the park, I felt like I had done my part. It had been months since I had exercised properly. Now that I was jobless, I could take care of my health a little better. Walks through the park was a great start.

The walk also helped clear my mind for a while.

Though, once I exited the trail and walked leisurely around the park, frustration knocked on my door again. Unfortunately, walking wouldn't solve my problem. I needed to go looking for a job. At this point, anything would do. I couldn't stay jobless for long, or soon I would be homeless too. Despite not liking my roommate, it was better than sleeping on the park's cold benches.

I heard a soft *woof* and looked down. A beautiful, small golden retriever puppy jumped in front of me, clearly excited to be at the park, but also clearly lost.

"Hey, little boy, where is your mommy?" I crouched down to pet him and glanced around. It was in the middle of the morning. I hadn't come to the park at this hour before, but I wasn't surprised it was empty. Adults should be at work, and kids should be at school. "Are you lost?"

The puppy let out another adorable *woof*. I couldn't leave him here. With gentle hands, I picked the puppy up and started walking around the park, looking for his owners.

I walked past a couple and an elderly woman, but when I asked, they said the puppy wasn't theirs. Finally, I found a little girl seated at a bench with her mother, sobbing her eyes out.

"I've lost him, Mommy," the little girl cried. "Now he's gone."

"He's not gone," I said, walking up to them. "Just

temporarily misplaced. I believe this pretty puppy is yours." I extended the puppy to her, my hands carefully wrapped across his torso.

The little girl's eyes became two big balls as she jumped off the bench and wrapped her arms around her puppy as if he was the most precious thing in the world. "Toby!" she screamed, squeezing him.

The girl's mother turned to me. "From what she described, I thought someone had taken him from her. I thought she would never see him again. How can I ever thank you?"

I shrugged. "It's okay. I just saw him alone and thought he was missing his mommy. Glad I could help."

The mother and girl thanked me again before I walked away. I had been in a bad mood after my walk, but now I felt good again. My life could be in shambles, I might not have money to buy anymore groceries, pay for lunch, or my rent, but at least I would go down with a sense of duty, like I had done my part to make this a better world.

Just outside the park, an elderly man was crouched on the sidewalk. Afraid he had fallen and was hurt, I crouched beside him. "What happened? Are you okay?"

His gray eyes met mine. "I-I'm fine, dear," he said, his voice frail and quivering almost as much as his hand. "I just dropped my wallet." He showed the empty black leather wallet to me. "I'm picking up my things." Just then I saw all the things around him: coins, bills, credit cards, health insurance card, and his ID.

I gulped at the sight of the thick wad of money about to blow away in the gentle breeze. Just a fraction of this money could pay for my rent and my groceries for the next month, maybe more. I didn't understand why he carried so much money around, but my heart squeezed when I helped him pick it up and handed it all to him.

"T-Thank you, dear," he said, as I helped him get up. He fished a hundred-dollar bill from his wallet and offered it to me. "Here. For helping me."

I confess, I felt tempted to snatch it, but it wasn't fair. I hadn't done more than just help him for thirty seconds. I didn't deserve money for that. Besides, this could be all this man had. Things weren't easy for the elderly, not in this country.

"It's okay." I pushed the bill back to him. "I'm sure you can make better use of that."

He thanked me again, and I dashed away, afraid that if I stayed any longer, I would succumb and accept his offer—which, honestly, would be like stealing candy from a baby.

I hurried back to my apartment, though halfway there I stopped. What would I do there? Mope? Cry? Search for a job that didn't exist?

Instead, I decided to walk some more, this time around town. It had been a while since I had walked without any real direction and purpose. Besides, the more I walked, the more tired I would feel later, and that would help me sleep better that night.

I walked down some known streets and shops, greeting some faces I had met at the restaurant before, until I saw the old dance studio that had closed a few months ago. The façade had been redone, and it was now called The Red House, a gentlemen's club. The sign on the door indicated they would open next week.

And they were hiring.

I halted and stared at the sign.

Could I work at a gentlemen's club? What did that entail?

If I didn't go in and ask, I would never know. Hopefully they'd need a bartender or a waitress. With my previous experience, I could do that, couldn't I? I thought I could.

But if they didn't, if the job they had an opening for was of something more...then I wasn't sure. I guess I had to hear the job description in detail, the payment, and the benefits. I had to weigh the pros and cons. I mean, what if I had to dance on a stage in a skimpy outfit? It wasn't what I wanted for me, but that would be better than being homeless, right?

Besides, I didn't need to do this forever. I just needed to save some money, or do this until I found something better, something more me.

Right?

Right?

I swallowed hard.

And then I stepped through the front door.

5

CADE

I HADN'T SLEPT in well over thirty hours, and from what I could see of Amber, she hadn't either. If she had, then it had been short naps between her outings.

Like a frosting creep, I followed Amber all morning.

I didn't know why I was doing this to myself. I should just grab her and go back to Wyth, to the White City. That would certainly be easier than watching her walking around, being nice and helping strangers...waking up a protective feeling inside my cold chest.

Snow above, why did she have to be so nice? I saw when a teenage boy took the dog from the little girl and ran with it. When I stopped him with my magic, the puppy ran away— right to Amber's arms. And as the pure-hearted soul she was, she walked around until she found the dog's owner.

Then there was the old man. She could have stolen money from him. I was certain most humans would. The old man would never know. But she didn't. And when he offered to pay her for her kindness, she refused.

Who in the freezing snow did that?

She was taking this whole selfless thing to an entirely new level.

I was sure I had seen it all from her. Then she shocked me when she stopped in front of that gentlemen's club. I knew what those were. I had been to one long ago, in one of my few visits to the human world. Most of what went on inside was just sexy games and play, but sometimes it turned into more.

I felt as if lightning had struck me down when she inhaled deeply and went inside the place.

What in the frost?

The protective feeling came back with a vengeance, bringing some rage and possessiveness with it. Seeing red, I went after her and marched inside the gentlemen's club.

The place was mostly empty—there was a man stocking drinks behind the bar, a woman wiping tables, and right in the center of it all, a man in a suit talking to Amber.

"I was a waitress at a local restaurant," she said, her voice strained, as if she was forcing the words out.

That was it. I was done playing.

I stomped to them, closed my hand around her wrist, and pulled her out of there.

"Hey!" she screamed, jerking against my hold. "What's going on? Who are you?" She used her other hand to try and pry mine off. Such a futile attempt. "Hey, are you deaf?"

Once we were outside, I let go of her wrist. Like a predator, I turned to her, hovering just half a foot from her. Her breath caught, and she shuffled backward, her huge eyes meeting mine.

A growl started low in my chest.

I had been following her since yesterday, and I had seen her many times. Since I first laid eyes on her, I noticed she was a beautiful woman. But until being this close to her, breathing in the same air as her, feeling the energy emanating from her body, and seeing all the details of her face, I hadn't realized she was more than beautiful.

She was stunning.

Her long, black hair danced behind her back, and her big, green eyes seemed to shine with a light of their own. Delicate nose and brows, pink lips, and a long neck, with smooth, fair skin that seemed to call to me, begging me to taste it.

Close like this, I could hear the sharp intake of her breathing and the palpitation of her heart. I could see the vein in her throat pulsing. I could smell the soft, sweet lavender scent of the perfume on her skin. I could feel the heat coming from her tight body—and I wanted to touch it all. Her lean legs, thin waist, generous hips, and even more generous breasts.

All she was missing was slightly pointed ears and, as humans would say, she would give any female fae a run for their money.

And my freezing body knew that. It instantly reacted to her; the blood in my veins warmed, and my core trembled with want.

For a moment, all I could think of was throwing her against the wall and ravishing her.

Blinking, Amber took another step back and crossed her arms. She raised her chin, clearly faking a bravado she didn't have. "Who the hell are you?"

This was just too much; not to mention I was wasting time. By now, the curse would have advanced further over my land. I had to put a stop to this before it reached any of the villages and harmed my people.

"I'm sorry about this," I told her.

Her brows pinched down. "Sorry about—"

I sent my magic swirling around her, the wind circling her, cutting off her words and her breathing. In three seconds, she fainted. I dropped my magic, and as her body folded to the ground, I slid my arms under her and pulled her against me.

She seemed so small in my arms, so fragile, so innocent.

A little guilt snaked through me.

But I pushed it away.

It was her or my court.

There was no question here.

I PACED AROUND MY STUDY.

I had been back from the human realm for a few hours. After depositing Amber's limp body into one of the guest chambers, I had assigned her a couple of handmaids and guards, then retreated to my study, where I knew *she* would find me.

Though, when she showed up, she wasn't the gentle Mahaera. The goddess had come as Mahaeru, the solemn and harsh one.

"I see you've brought her with you," Mahaeru said. Her black hair was tied in a tight bun at the nape of her neck, and her clothes were dark and practical, so unlike her other sisters.

"So, when can we do the ritual?" I asked, eager to get this over with. If it depended on me, I would remain in my study, oblivious to everything while Mahaeru and her other two selves conducted everything.

Mahaeru stared at me with hard eyes. "It doesn't work like that. First, the human needs to be cleansed."

"What? Cleansed? What in the frost do you mean?"

"What did I tell you about saving your people?" she asked, her tone flat.

Why did they do this to me? Mahaera, Mahaere, and Mahaeru were goddesses of Wyth. They were the most powerful and wise beings that ever set foot in the fae realm. No one would dare challenge them, question them.

And yet, when one of them asked me something like that, I wondered if they were playing with me. Tricking me.

"Mahaera told me that I needed to find a selfless, pure-hearted human, and during a complicated ritual, sacrifice her life. That should be enough to stop the curse." Other than me, only Kei had heard Mahaera's words. No one else knew about it.

Mahaeru nodded. "It should be, but the human needs to be prepared. Everything in Wyth is different than on Earth, including this. If this human isn't cleansed before her sacrifice, it won't change anything."

I clenched my fists until they turned white. "How long will that take?"

"Two weeks, I think," Mahaeru said.

"Two weeks? By then my court will be half gone!" I barked.

"Alas, it's the only way," Mahaeru said, remaining coldly calm. "Send her to the Moon Temple every morning, and I'll conduct the cleansing. I'll let you know when she's ready to be sacrificed for your kingdom."

I swallowed hard.

When Mahaera had first told me about the sacrifice, I didn't blink. I didn't think twice. A meaningless human life for my entire court? That was nothing. Now, I wasn't sure I liked that idea.

But I had no choice.

To save my land from the curse poisoning it, I had to kill Amber.

I faced the goddess, my will turning into steel. "She'll be there tomorrow morning."

6

AMBER

I OPENED MY EYES, but it seemed I was still dreaming. Sitting up, I studied the soft, white blanket over my legs. And this dress? I smoothed my hands on the silky fabric of the beautiful white gown I was wearing. Stunned, I looked around. Was I some sort of princess in this dream? Because this place...it was out of this world.

The bed was probably bigger than a king size, with a tall headboard covered in white velvet. The nightstands flanking the bed were bigger than my puny desk in my apartment. I scooted to the edge of the bed and put my legs down. My bare feet sank in the soft, thick, white rug.

On the other side of the bedroom were a tall, round table and two armchairs—also all white. Everything was either white or silver here.

Long, heavy curtains covered one of the walls. I went to them and pulled them open. Bright light filtered through the wide window. I blinked once, twice, then glanced out.

My jaw fell open.

My eyes fixed on the view below, I pushed the windows

open. A chilly breeze blew in, and I hugged myself, but I couldn't stop staring at the world beyond the window.

A dull, bluish-yellow sun illuminated the vast, cloudless, light-blue sky. In the distance stood a wide forest and large mountains, all covered in a blanket of white snow. And right below the window was what looked like a village. A white, gray, and silver village that reminded me of some medieval movie, though cleaner. Neater. Whiter.

"It's cold out," a rough voice said. "You should close the windows."

I turned around and faced the man standing in front of white double doors. I blinked, now certain this was a dream, because, holy shit, I had never seen a more manly and sexy man in all my life. He was tall and wide and, more importantly, shirtless. His chest and stomach were sculpted to perfection, the ridges of each muscle deep. He wore a white leather strap across his chest, which tied to the long, white cloak on his back, giving him an air of superiority. Other than that, he wore simple white pants and a thick silver belt, which fitted his impossibly large thighs in a way that should be R rated.

"How are you feeling?" he asked, drawing my attention to his face.

I opened my mouth to answer, but my thoughts zoomed in on him again, so this time, I stared at his handsome, rugged face. Like his body, I had never seen a more beautiful face. His bright, luminous blue eyes were the first thing that snatched my attention. I had never seen eyes like those. Along with a sharp nose, pouted lips, thick eyebrows, sharp chin, and a chiseled jaw, this man was like a god brought to life.

Or brought to my dreams.

The finishing touch was the long white hair falling over the cloak around his shoulders. Yup, in this dream, this man was either a god or a warrior—though it could all be summed up in one way: if he was here, then it was for me.

A small smile stretched over my lips. "I'm more than fine now."

Kimberly had always teased me about being a prude, and in real life that might be true, but not in my dreams. I was twenty-one, for goodness sake. I wasn't stupid. I had seen TV shows with explicit sex scenes, and I had read lots of steamy romance books, so I knew a lot about it, and I had practice with it—in my dreams.

And now I had conjured a new boy toy for me, one who would put all the others to shame.

"I'm feeling great," I said, surrendering to the dream. With my eyes locked on his, I walked toward him, moving my hips more than I would in a normal situation. I slid my hand down from my shoulder, across my chest, around my waist. His eyes followed my hand, becoming bluer and brighter with each passing second. "I'm more than great, actually."

I halted just half a foot from him. Holy shit, he was an entire head taller than me. I bet he could wrap his arms around me, and I would disappear in him. Hm, I wanted to try that theory. I bit my lower lip, and his gaze shifted to my mouth. I reached up, resting my palms on the hard planes of his chest.

Heat seeped into my hands, up my arms, and down to my core. That heat quickly consumed me, turning into pure lust, and pooling low in my belly.

I turned my chin up and rose on my tiptoes. "What do you want to do with me?" I asked in a low voice before brushing my lips across his chin and—

The man let out a menacing growl before stepping back.

I lost my balance and almost face planted at his feet.

"Amber, what are you doing?"

I stared at the man, stunned. "What the hell are *you* doing? This is my damn dream and—"

"This isn't a dream."

I froze. What? How could this not be a dream? I glanced down at the gown I was wearing, at his clothes directly out of a romance book, and this bedroom. I was sure this was inside a castle, a castle where I was the princess and he was the warrior tasked to protect me.

"How...?" My eyes widened, and I sucked in a sharp breath when I finally remembered him. He had been wearing different clothes, and his hair had been tied back in a low ponytail, but I was sure it was him—the man who had dragged me out of the gentlemen's club. The man who said he was sorry before I blacked out. And ended up here? Inside my head, right, because.... "This has to be a dream," I muttered.

"It's not a dream," the man repeated, his voice rougher than before. Lower.

I took a step back. "It has to be." I reached for my arm and pinched myself, hissing as the pain spread through my arm.

"I told you it isn't a dream."

Holy shit. If that was the truth, then two things made me equally afraid and embarrassed. One, if this wasn't a dream, then it meant this man had kidnapped me and had me in one of his crazy fantasies, and two, I had just thrown myself at him as if I was a slut.

And he had refused me.

Heat spread over my cheeks, and I looked down, wishing a hole would open up in the ground so I could hide in it.

"I-If this isn't a dream, then where I am?" I held on to the fear, the wariness, and put on a fake bravado. I wouldn't let my own shame hide what was really happening here. I didn't know this place or this man. I wanted to get out of here right now. "Who are you, and what have you done to me?"

I quickly glanced around, taking everything in with a new thought in mind: escape routes. The window was too freaking high, and the other two doors I saw led to a closet and a gigantic bathroom. The only other option was the double doors behind the man.

"I know how this seems," he said, his voice a little gentler than a moment ago. "This place looks impossible, and you're alone in here, thinking I'll probably hurt you." He swallowed hard. "I assure you, you're safe here."

"Said every kidnapper ever," I mumbled.

"Here." He took a step forward and puffed out his chest, becoming even taller and bigger than before. Holy shit. "My name is Cadewyn, and I'm the king of the Winter Court in Wyth."

I shook my head. "King? Winter Court? That sounds right out of a fairy tale, and you want me to believe that?"

"I know, I know it sounds insane to a human, but—"

"To a human? What are you then?"

"I'm a fae."

I laughed. "You're telling me that you are a fairy?"

"No, that's different." He reached up, brushing his hand over my eyes and my mouth. I slapped his hand away. "What the hell?" I blinked, my vision a little blurred. "What did you do to me?"

"I've given you the speech and the sight. Give it a moment; you'll be able to speak my language and your vision will stabilize, and then you'll see things you couldn't before." He ran his hand over his hair, tucking some strands behind his ear—his pointed ear.

"You're...." I rubbed at my eyes, sure I was seeing things. "You really are a fairy."

"I said that's different. I'm fae. We're in Wyth, the faerie realm."

I started pacing and pressed my fingertips on my temple, feeling a headache coming. "This is crazy. This is absurd."

"Listen, what language am I speaking?"

I stared at him. Holy shit, he wasn't speaking English anymore and I was understanding him! "What the hell?" I slapped my mouth, as the same language came out of my mouth. "What freakish thing is this? This can't be real!"

"I'm not going to argue with you about what's real and what isn't," Cadewyn said. "I'm just going to tell you how it is. We're in Wyth, the faerie realm. There are eight courts in Wyth, the Winter Court is one of them, and I'm its king."

I halted and faced him, both scared and angry about whatever shit was going on here. "And what does that have to do with me? Why the hell am I here?"

"I'm sorry for kidnapping you, but I had no choice," he said, his voice low. The sudden softness in his eyes...it was as if he really meant it. "I was desperate. I brought you here because I need your help."

My brows arched up. "What kind of help?"

CADE

SNOW ABOVE....

How could I tell Amber the truth? Just a moment ago she was lost in a fantasy world in her head, where she tried to kiss me.

And I almost let her. When she sauntered up to me, her green eyes fixed on mine, her sensual body moving toward me. Then she stopped right in front of me and touched me, her lips grazing my chin....

I almost lost it. I almost surrendered to the lust igniting my insides and demanding that I throw her on the bed and taste her. Have her. Eat her alive.

But it wasn't right.

As much as I wanted to surrender to the desire that was starting to drive me crazy, I couldn't. I wasn't supposed to be so enthralled by her, so shaken by her, so ensnared in her web.

I was supposed to kill her. To ask her to die for my court.

How in the freezing ice would I tell her that?

"In two weeks, there will be a big event," I told her, trying to insert as much truth as I could in my lie. "You need to take part in this event so we can save my land."

Her delicate brows slanted down. "Save your land? From what?"

I hadn't considered showing her the curse, but now that she had asked that, I wondered if it wasn't a good idea. If she saw what we were up against, then maybe she would feel honored to take part in said "event" and not hate me as much when she learned the truth.

Besides, I hadn't checked on the curse since I came back from the human world. I wanted to know how far it had advanced.

I extended my hand to her. "I can show you."

Amber watched my hand, still wary of me. I couldn't blame her. To humans, the fae realm, our appearance, and our magic seemed absurd. And being here, finding out this wasn't a dream, and having to trust a stranger? All that would be difficult for her.

"I would rather just go home," she said, her voice tight. "Can I help you from there?"

I shook my head once. "You can't, but here is a deal. Why don't you come with me and let me show you what you'll be saving us from? If after seeing it you still want to go home, then I'll take you."

It was a risky gamble, but one I took, betting on what I had seen of her in the thirty hours I had followed her. Amber was the selfless and pure-hearted human Mahaera had told me about, I was sure of that. I just hoped she would be selfless about my land and my people too. If she saw the curse with her own eyes, she wouldn't resist it. She would want to help.

"Why should I believe you?" she asked. "You could be

lying to me."

"True, but would that change anything? You're still in this room, and I know you know you can't overpower me and escape. Stay locked in here or at least come outside with me."

She winced. "When you put it that way...."

I outstretched my hand to her again. "What do you say?"

She hesitated but ended up slipping her hand in mine. I folded my hand around hers, intrigued by how small and delicate it was—just like all of her.

That same, deep protective feeling I had before stirred in my chest. I frowned, not liking the thoughts and emotions it was bringing forth.

I stepped back and gestured to the door. "This way."

NOBODY BOTHERED us when we left the guest chambers and walked through the palace hallways. We strolled past a few guards and servants, and they all stopped and bowed to me.

Meanwhile, Amber stared at everyone and everything in her way. I tried putting myself in her shoes and imagined I was seeing the White Palace for the first time.

The palace was grandiose and powerful. With wide corridors, big arches, tall ceilings, heavy ice chandeliers, smooth white floors, and long, tall windows, it was sure intimidating. But to me, it had always been my home.

And beyond it were my people.

We made it to the doors leading to the back garden, where the stables were. I thought we were safe; then her voice rang through the walls.

"Where are you going?" Chiara asked.

I turned to my little sister. She wasn't as little anymore,

but to me, she would always be a child. I loved her, but since the death of our father many years ago, she had turned quiet and lonely, and I didn't know what to do to reach her.

"Chiara, this is Amber." I gestured from one woman to the other. "Amber, this is Chiara, my sister."

Chiara glided across the floor as if she walked on a cloud, her steps long and precise. As the winter princess, she carried the traits of our people: white hair, light-blue eyes, fair skin. She was tall and slender, but from what Kei told me, her delicate form and movements were just the princess in her. She was getting more agile and stronger during her combat training lessons.

"Oh, the human," my sister said. She looked at me, and I arched an eyebrow. Chiara didn't know the real reason Amber was here. Only Kei knew that. All the others just thought the same as Amber: that I needed her for a ceremony. After that, we didn't need her anymore. "Welcome to the Winter Court."

"Thank you," Amber said, her voice low. She was openly staring at my sister, probably still taking in the fact that we were fae and not humans.

Chiara glanced at me. "You didn't answer my question."

"I'm taking Amber to see the curse," I said simply.

Chiara dipped her chin in a nod. "I see you forgot she's human."

I frowned. What in the frost was she talking about?

"One moment." Chiara disappeared into a room on the left, which led to the servants' quarters underground. A moment later, she came up with a heavy, white fur coat in her hands and handed it to Amber. "You'll be cold without the proper clothing."

I had forgotten about that. Though my body was warm,

like humans, the cold was part of who I was. The Winter Court people didn't feel cold easily. In fact, we thrived when it was the coldest.

Chiara helped Amber put on the coat and pulled its hood over her head.

"Thank you," Amber said, looking like an ice queen with that coat on. The dark hair contrasted with her fair skin and the white of the fur. Like this, her green eyes looked incredibly bright. I ached to touch her.

"I'll let you go now," Chiara said.

I stripped my gaze from Amber and cleared my throat. "Right." I beckoned to the door behind us. "This way." After a quick wave to Chiara, Amber followed me out. The six White Knights immediately fell into step with us, startling Amber. "Don't mind them," I told her, but she didn't seem very convinced.

I guided her to the stables, where I had a servant boy help me get Blizzard, my horse, ready.

"Hm, we're taking a horse?" Amber asked, sounding unsure. "Where are you taking me, and, um...can we take a car?"

I almost laughed at that. "We don't have cars here. We have carriages, but if we go by horseback, it'll be faster." Though the border was eight hours away. To make it a little faster, I would infuse my magic in Blizzard's powerful legs.

"But...this horse is huge."

"Don't worry." I had to keep in mind that everything was different here, even the horses. Here, the horses were taller and larger than in the human world. Stronger and faster too. "I know Blizzard looks intimidating, but he's a good horse." When Blizzard was ready, I hopped on top of him and extended my hand to her. "I'll keep you safe, I promise." *At least for now.* Still looking a little unsure, Amber took my hand, and I hoisted her up right behind me. She held on to the coat, keeping her hands occupied. "Trust me, you'll want to hang on." I reached behind me, took her hands in mine, and brought her arms around me. "If you don't, you will fall."

My stomach knotted with desire as her warm hands splayed over my abdomen. Then I heard her suck in a sharp breath, which only ignited my lust.

Snow above, this way we wouldn't get anywhere.

Trying my hardest to ignore the woman currently holding on to me, I kicked Blizzard's sides and off we went. At first, I guided my horse to a slow trot, so Amber could see the White Palace as we rounded the grounds, the extensive snow garden in the front with its many ice sculptures, the massive ice gates, and beyond it the White City.

The town sprawled around the palace's outer walls, with its quaint houses and familiar shops. I pointed out certain places to her as we trotted through the main road—the open theater, the marketplace, the restaurant with the best honey cakes I had ever tasted. And along the way, I greeted my people.

They bowed their heads to me, but they gawked at Amber. I knew what they were thinking; the single king with a female? That had to be a miracle.

If only they knew the truth....

"Everyone has the same features," Amber mused, her mouth near my shoulder. To her, the several fae with white or blond hair, fair skin, and blue or gray eyes was probably alarming. To me, it was the only thing I knew.

"You'll see a fae or two with different features around town and even in the palace, but it's because they either came from another court and settled here, or because they are the offspring of a Winter Court fae with a fae from a different court," I explained.

"I see."

Soon, we crossed the village's main gates and onto the main road that cut through the entire court.

"Hold on tight," I warned before sending my magic to Blizzard and kicking his sides again.

The horse shot forward, heading south. Amber yelped, her long nails scratching my stomach as she tried to hold on. It stung a little, but the pain was quickly replaced by something else, something I didn't want to admit. Something I needed to suppress.

The trip to the border didn't take long, even though I slowed down when we were passing through landmarks or other villages, so Amber could see more of the Winter Court and what she would be helping me with. What she would be saving.

Halfway there, I purposely steered Blizzard off the road near a frozen lake and showed Amber some of the magical beings that lived there.

Amber stared at them with big eyes. "What are those?"

"Frost sprites," I told her, watching the female-like creatures dancing around the lake. They had long, shimmering bodies usually covered by a skimpy white or silver dress, and hair in several shades of blue. "They are tied to the nature of the Winter Court. Their magic prospers if the land prospers." Which meant, if the land continued dying, the frost sprites would lose their magic. If not die.

Amber hadn't recovered from her shock of seeing the frost sprites when we came across a snow fox. Half-hidden behind a leafless tree, the fox kept its white eyes on us. Its white fur glowed under the sunlight, making it look just as magical as it was.

"I've never seen a white fox before," Amber whispered.

"Snow foxes are powerful magical beings, but very wary of others," I said. "Do you see how immobile it is? It won't move until we're gone. Unless we advance toward it, then it'll run away."

We gazed at the fox for a minute more, and then continued our trek.

It had been only two days since I had last been at the border, but the curse had advanced more than I expected. I caught sight of one of my army's legions from a distance, the soldiers all standing as a barrier in front of our most current enemy: the curse.

"What's happening?" Amber asked, spying over my shoulder.

"You'll see," I said, my voice as tight as my chest. I slowed our pace as we approached the new border.

The legion saw us coming and turned to us, lowering their heads at me.

Kei stepped forward. "Welcome back, my king."

My eyes on the black horizon, I dismounted. For a moment, I even forgot why I had come here, who I had brought with me, because all I could see and think and feel was the expanse of land in front of me.

Or what was left of it.

The darkness spread until it disappeared beyond trees—trees that were now as black and dead as the ground.

The legion stepped back as I walked forward, going for the poisoned area.

"Stay back," I heard Kei caution. "It's dangerous."

Frowning, I turned around and saw Amber standing between Kei and me.

Amber.

I had brought her here to show this to her. Would she feel the same desperation I felt when I explained to her what this was? Would she feel compelled to help, no matter the price?

Was she truly that selfless?

"Come." I gestured for her to advance toward me.

With sure steps, Amber walked until she was right by my side. "What is this?" she asked, her voice low, her eyes on the dead horizon.

"This is a curse," I told her. "The border is a couple of miles that way." I pointed straight ahead of us. "It started there. A curse sent by the Tabred clan, one of our enemies."

"Tabred? I'm not following."

"Beyond the border is a place called Tywyll Forest, which is inhabited by monsters. No main leader, no real organization, no care for the land or for others. Just some greedy, vicious monsters. Some of them got together and created clans, so they could try to become more powerful. One of these clans is called Tabred. Since their hideout is near our border, they started a war against us a long time ago." I gulped, uncomfortable reliving these memories. "They killed my father, and I was crowned king. Right after, I organized a strategic attack on them. I killed all of their important figures and leaders and their commander. And his family. After that, we had peace." I let out a long breath. "At least until recently, when we learned I mistakenly left the commander's son alive, Grimmel. He vowed to get his revenge on me. I thought he was going to restart the war, but he didn't. I became tense, waiting for his attack. Months passed, and it didn't come." I opened my arms, indicating the view ahead of us. "Until this."

"Grimmel poisoned your land," Amber said, her voice low and sympathetic.

"Yes. A cursed poison that is spreading and will consume everything and everyone in its path. I tried using my magic to stop it, but it doesn't budge. The only thing that will stop it is a special event." I turned to her, hating myself for having to lie again. "A ceremony, actually, in which you'll play an important part."

"Why me?" she asked.

"Because you're a pure-hearted, selfless human."

Amber scoffed. "Pure-hearted? Selfless? Me?"

I frowned. Didn't she know that? I had been around her for two entire days now and even I knew that. "Yes, you. The most pure-hearted and selfless person, human or fae, that I ever met."

She blinked, as if I was telling her something absurd. "Well, I'm sure you're mistaken, but why not? We can try it. Worst thing that will happen is for it not to work, right? When can we do it?"

I shook my head. "It doesn't work like that," I told her. At least I wouldn't be lying about this part. "You have to undergo a cleansing ritual every morning for two weeks before we do this."

Amber's mouth fell open. "Two weeks?"

"Believe me, I don't want to wait either." I gestured to the cursed land again. "This is what happened in two days, and for this ritual to work, we'll have to wait another two weeks."

"But...." Her eyes searched mine.

"We made a deal," I continued. "If I showed you what you would be helping us with and you still wanted to go home, I said I would take you." I hang on to her nature, hoping I was right about her. "Can you look me in the eye and say that you can leave just like that after seeing this?" I pointed to the dark land just a few feet from us. "It's just for two weeks. Please."

Amber looked at the poisoned land, then back at me. I could see her conflict stamped in her pretty eyes. Then her shoulders sagged. "All right. It's not like I have anything to do back at home anyway."

I let out a long, relieved breath. She had bought it. I knew she wouldn't be able to resist it once she saw the land, once she understood what it would do to my people.

But because of that, I felt a pit called guilt opening deep in my chest.

THERE WERE moments when I still thought I was dreaming.

For example, when Cade—I had heard the general calling him that when no one else seemed to be listening—took me riding on his giant horse through an impossibly beautiful icy land. When he showed me the curse infecting his land. When he took me back to the palace as the sun went down, bathing the White Palace in bluish silver light, making it shine so bright, I couldn't look directly to it.

That night, Chiara had come to my room with a tray full of delicious food.

"Fae food is tricky," she said. "Eat only what Cade or I give to you. Understand?"

I asked what she meant, but she didn't elaborate. I confess I was intimidated by Chiara. She looked like a model who belonged on a Victoria's Secret runway. Tall, slim but with the right curves, long silver hair, the smoothest skin, and the bluest eyes I had ever seen. Despite all that, she was guarded, stoic, and so sure of herself. She didn't speak more than necessary and looked at me as if I was a frail human who needed constant care. I was sure she didn't do it on purpose. It was just her way.

After dinner, Chiara introduced me to two handmaids who would take care of me while I was with them: Tania and Zari—two young fae girls, very pretty but very shy too. They wanted to do everything for me from drawing a bath, scrubbing me, brushing my teeth, to choosing my nightgown, dressing me, and tucking me in bed.

I didn't allow them to do anything other than sit in the two armchairs by the table and relax. I wasn't some silly, helpless princess, and I wasn't going to start acting like one now. As much as I liked the comfort, the great scenery, the amazing food, and the luscious gowns, I didn't want to get addicted to this. In two weeks, I would go back home to my shitty apartment, even shittier roommate, and no job.

I had expressed a concern to Cade on the way back from the border. "I need to warn Kimberly that I'll be away for two weeks. If I don't, she'll sell my things and find herself a new roommate."

He had assured me he would send someone to let her know I was away on a trip and would soon be back. That made me feel better. I hated that apartment, that entire life, but it was the only one I had.

The next morning, Chiara showed up with a breakfast fit for a queen. The tray was brimming with food, most of which I had never seen in my life, and even though I couldn't eat it all, I tasted a bite of everything. There were two items I didn't particularly like—the saffron fish cakes, and the old bark tea —but the rest was amazing, especially the warm honey cakes. Tania, who had stayed after Chiara left, had told me the name of each dish, but it was too much in too little time. I couldn't remember all of it even if my life depended on it.

After breakfast, Tania took me to the grand foyer on the palace's first floor.

There, I met Mahaera.

When the female fae smiled at me, I just knew she was more than a normal fae. She seemed older than me, around mid-thirties, but I was sure that wasn't her age. There was wisdom and power behind her gentle eyes and easy smile. Her white hair was tied in a loose braid over her shoulder, and she wore a simple white gown that on her seemed fit for a queen.

"I'm here to take you to the cleansing ritual, my dear," she said, her voice even and reassuring. She offered me her arm. "Come with me."

I hesitated, only because I didn't know her. Well, I didn't know anyone here, not really, but so far I trusted Cade, and he had told me to trust Chiara. He had also told me to go with Mahaera when she came for me.

When I took her arm, she knotted my hand around her elbow, then tugged me along with her. She guided me through the palace's hallways, through a door that led to a wide covered porch, past a long stone path cleared of snow where the cold wind blew by and chilled my bones, past some tall, snowcapped bushes, and to a round, white building.

"What is this place?" I asked, still lost on all things fae.

"This is the Moon Temple," she said as she guided me in. "It's a sacred place where we can worship the magic of the land."

That didn't make much sense to me, but I quickly forgot my confusion as I stared at the place. Inside was just as simple as the outside—just a large, round room with a pool in the middle. A handful of other female fae stood around the pool, all of them with a drawing of a white crescent moon on their foreheads. "And these are the priestesses. They will help us with the cleansing ritual."

I looked around, as if searching for a tool, a machine, maybe some books. There was nothing here. "Hm, and what do I have to do for this ritual?"

Mahaera took me to the edge of the pool. "You need to undress and enter the pool."

My eyes bugged. "What?"

Mahaera let out a soft chuckle. "I know humans don't normally bare themselves like that, but here, it's not that uncommon for us. Don't worry too much about it."

I stared at the water before me. "Can't I just go in with my dress?"

"I assure you, we have seen it all before." She let go of me. "Now, please, let's start." She took a step back and looked at me expectantly.

I glanced at the fae around me, suddenly wary of this whole thing. Wasn't I really dreaming still? I had to be. A fae world, a devastating curse, stunning people, and now a ritual that required me to be naked. Next, I would see myself naked in the middle of the street in Brooksville with people laughing at me.

But this wasn't a dream, was it? I had been here for over twenty-four hours. I had seen too much, done too much. I had even pinched myself, gone to sleep, and woke up—and I was still here.

And there was only one way to go home: I had to help these fae.

So, with my stomach in knots, I took off my fur coat, pulled down the straps of my white gown, and let it fall to my feet. Cautiously, I stepped into the water. It was warmer than

I expected, and it was shallow at first, but the bottom was steep, and soon I was standing in the middle of the pool with the water by my shoulders.

"What do I do now?" I asked.

"Just relax," Mahaera said.

Around the pool, Mahaera and the other females joined hands. They closed their eyes and began chanting in a language I didn't understand.

I felt exposed and awkward in the pool, while these beautiful fae sang and swayed side to side. The warm water heated slightly, and a bright white light showed up at the bottom of the pool. I stepped back, but the light spread through the water, as if it was coming from everywhere. It tingled against my skin, making me hotter and lightheaded.

"Mahaera," I whispered as my vision blurred.

"It's okay, my dear," she said from somewhere above me. "Just surrender."

I didn't want to. I didn't like this. I didn't feel in control, but right then, I didn't have much choice. Whatever this was, it was much stronger than me. I couldn't resist it.

The light shone bright, the tingling spread all over me, and the water heated some more.

I slipped underwater.

I blinked and saw Mahaera's smile right in front of me. "Are you okay, my dear?" she asked, her voice serene.

Confused, I glanced down at myself. I was dressed in my gown, but my hair was still wet. "What happened?" I asked, noticing the female fae were on the other side of the temple, talking to each other. How had I gone from the pool to standing here all dressed?

"You surrendered to the cleanse," she said, handing me

the heavy fur coat. "It's all done for today." She gestured to the entrance of the temple. "You can go now."

I frowned. That was it? She wouldn't take me back to the palace herself? I was allowed to walk by myself? Well, it wasn't as if I was a prisoner, was it? I was here to help, and then I would be sent home.

Home.

I wasn't sure I had one of those anymore. Or if I had ever had one.

Suddenly sad, I walked out of the temple. I pulled the hood of the fur coat over my head and tugged it tighter against me. This damn cold.... This kingdom was beautiful, at least the little bits I had seen so far, but I didn't think I could ever get used to the cold.

Halfway along the stone path that led back to the palace, I halted.

Cade stood in my way.

I inhaled sharply as I stared at him. With the snow blanketing the ground and the palace right behind him, he looked like a painting, one of a powerful god who took my breath away every time I laid eyes on him.

The wind blew around us, whipping his long, white hair behind his back and moving the edges of his long cloak. I knew he was the freaking king of winter, or whatever, but couldn't he put on a damn shirt when he was outside? One, it was too cold—I didn't care if he didn't feel cold like I did; seeing him like that made me colder. And two, it actually didn't. Seeing him like that made me hot, way too damn hot. Didn't he know by now that he could render me breathless with one glance, with one word?

"How was the ritual?" he asked, his rough voice drawing

me in. He took a few steps forward until he was only three feet from me.

"It was...interesting," I admitted. I was still confused about the entire thing. Fae rituals and magic didn't make any sense to me, so I couldn't really tell what was working or not. But if it really was necessary for the main ceremony in two weeks, then so be it. I didn't see any harm in spending my mornings with Mahaera and the other female fae.

"Yesterday, when we left to see the curse, I noticed you seemed very curious while we rode through White City," Cade said. "I was wondering if you would like to take a tour of the city with me."

I stared at him. "Hm, I would love to, but don't you have kingly stuff to do other than waste your time with me?"

His thick brows curled down. "I don't think that showing you my city and my people is a waste of time. I think you'll fall in love with this place and feel even better about helping out. That's certainly worth it."

A faint rush of excitement coursed through me. The silly girl in me liked the idea of being out with him way too much, because it was as if he was asking me out on a date. I hadn't been asked on too many dates before, and back home, I doubted a man like him would ever look at me.

I knew he was spending time with me and paying me attention because, apparently, I was the only one who could save his land from the curse; otherwise, he wouldn't even look at me twice, maybe not even once. But, for a couple of hours, I could pretend he did look at me. That he cared about me.

I shook my head once, pushing all these crazy thoughts away. It was too silly, too ridiculous. I had to think of this outing as a business meeting, nothing more.

"If you say so," I said, trying to sound mildly uninterested. I was sure it was all in vain.

Cade guided me to the stables again, where Blizzard was waiting for us, along with the six White Knights. He jumped on the horse effortlessly and pulled me up behind him. Once again, I was self-conscious of holding on to him, of touching his warm body and feeling the dozens of hard muscles under his skin. It was hard to focus on anything else this way.

The horse jolted forward, and I splayed my hands on Cade's stomach, holding on tight. Then, as the horse settled into a nice, slow trot, I buried my face in his back, mortally embarrassed.

Soon, we left the palace grounds and entered the city, but unlike yesterday, Cade steered the horse off the main road and went to the marketplace. At the main entrance, he brought Blizzard to a stop and hopped off. Then he helped me down by holding my hands.

The White Knights started dismounting.

Still holding my hand, Cade turned to them and said, "Don't stay too close."

The White Knights bowed their heads in acknowledgement.

Cade let go of my hand and beckoned me to come with him. By now, we had passed several fae, and they all stared, not only at their king but at me too. They were probably curious about what a human woman was doing here.

Once we entered the marketplace, I tried focusing on the beauty of the place, not the curious fae who turned to look at me.

I focused on the tall, ice-like dome that served as a roof for this long street and on the many stands with white, silver, or gray decorations. Some had more colorful items, like red, yellow, and green rings, scarves, or purses, but those were rare, and from the fae manning those stands, I gathered from their different skin and hair colors that they were foreigners in the Winter Court. But from the little I could see, the foreigners were treated as equals here.

Every two steps, Cade stopped and greeted his people. They all bowed to him in respect, making me wonder if I should do that too, if I should keep my distance from him. After all, he was a fae king, and I was an insignificant human.

Though he didn't smile—I didn't think I had ever seen him smiling—Cade seemed more relaxed and at ease than I had ever seen him. Some of the fae he knew by name. He stopped by a shoe stand and asked about the fae's wife. She had been sick last month, but now she was much better.

Cade really cared about his people, and that was quite heartwarming.

Surprising me, Cade stopped by a jewelry stand. He picked up beautiful earrings with dangling snowflakes at the end and brought them to the side of my face.

"I'll take these," he said to the stand owner. The fae insisted Cade take them for free, but Cade paid him anyway. Then, he handed them to me. "A gift."

I stared at the earrings, confused. Was there a meaning behind this gift? Why was he giving it to me? "Thank you," I whispered, taking the earrings from him.

As if nothing had happened, Cade moved on.

I stared at the earrings for a moment longer, admiring them and his kind gesture, then tucked them in the pocket of my coat and followed him.

As we went deeper into the marketplace, the stands changed from displaying jewelry and clothing to spices and food. A mix of sweet and spicy scents reached my nose, making my mouth water. Cade warned me to wait for him to tell me what I could eat or drink.

"Why can't I eat it all?" I asked, curious.

"Some food and drink act like strong drugs to humans," he said, his voice tight. "Others can make you lose your mind completely."

Well, that was scary as shit.

Cade handed me something that looked like cashews but tasted so sweet, it melted on my tongue. Then he offered an ice cup with a clear, smoking liquid. It looked like some kind of sparkling water, but when I drank it, I coughed as a burning sensation went down my throat. It reminded me of the only time I drank vodka and almost threw up after the first taste. But, after a moment, the burning was gone and a sweet and tangy taste replaced it.

"It's amazing," I said. It really was. Not just the drink, but everything. The great food, the myriad of scents, the elegant stands, the incredible setting, the content fae. It was all so impossible, so magical, I really felt like I had landed in a fairy tale.

We went on until the stands disappeared, giving way to what reminded me of a square. A group of fae played odd string instruments in a corner, while others danced and drank and chatted. Kids ran around, playing and laughing. And on one side, a group of fae displayed their magic. I stared in awe as they moved their hands, creating ice sculptures—birds, mermaids, trees. It was the first time I saw magic with my own eyes, and I suddenly felt so small, so insignificant. There were no words to describe what I had just seen.

"Come with me," Cade whispered, his mouth close to my ear. I shivered at his proximity. He entered a building to the side of the marketplace, and I followed him. "Through here," he said, taking the wide steps.

We climbed up a few flights of stairs until they ended at a door. Cade opened it and gestured for me to go on. Still a little wary, I did.

And gasped.

We were atop a building, on the roof. Ice railing lined the edge of the roof, and from here, I could see everything. The palace in the distance shining almost silver with the sunlight from the afternoon, the White City sprawling over a couple of miles, and down below the ice dome angled just right, showing off some of the marketplace underneath.

I leaned forward on the railing and breathed in deeply. For once, the cold wind didn't bother me. I glanced at Cade, standing right beside me. "Your city is beautiful," I told him with a small smile. "Everything here is beautiful. Thank you for showing this to me."

He fixed those brilliant blue eyes on mine. "My pleasure." He shuffled to the side until he was a foot from me. "I think they like you."

I blinked. "Who?"

"My people," he said, his voice hoarser than usual. "You know, I've never been seen, at least by them, with a female before. This is the second time in two days that I've shown up with you by my side. They probably think something is going on."

My cheeks heated, and I was sure I was becoming redder than a tomato. "Don't you have someone special?" I asked before I could stop myself—not that I didn't want to know, but that question did sound a little more than just me being curious, even to my own ears.

"No." His lips turned downward. "As a king, I shouldn't waste my time with relationships."

I frowned at that. So, what? The king was supposed to be alone?

"What I mean is, I shouldn't date for fun. About eighty percent of the fae find their mates when they're still young, so I should wait until I find mine."

My stomach dropped. So...he was waiting for his mate. That was very noble of him. Then why did I feel so betrayed by that?

"I hope you find her soon," I forced myself to say.

Cade nodded, and his brows slammed down. "Amber...," he whispered.

I practically leaned forward. "Yes?"

His gaze flickered to my lips. Was I seeing things? I had to be, right? Yesterday, when I thought it had all been a dream, he refused me, but right now he was looking at my lips as if he wanted to kiss me.

He reached over, brushing a loose strand of my hair back. His fingertips grazed my cheek, sending a delicious shiver down my spine, and I sucked in a sharp breath. "Amber, I—"

"My king." Someone rushed onto the roof. Cade took a large step back and faced the man. It was Kei, his general and best friend. "The curse, Cade. It has reached the Neige village."

Cade's face paled, as if that was even possible. "What?" He turned to me. "I'll send the White Knights to escort you back to the palace." Without another second to spare, he started after Kei.

"Wait," I called out. He paused and glanced at me. "Take me with you. I want to help."

Eyes sporting blue fire, Cade shook his head. "You'll be safer in the palace."

I opened my mouth to argue, but he was gone. I leaned over the rail and watched as he and Kei exited the building and rushed through the crowd, probably racing to get to his horse.

A moment later, a White Knight appeared at the roof's door. "I'll escort you back to the palace, my lady."

With a sigh, I followed the knight.

9

CADE

HALF OF NEIGE had been taken by the curse by the time I arrived there. My legions were working hard to help my people evacuate before they were hurt. Without hesitating, I took off my cloak and joined the fray. I carried elderly and children, while yelling for young and adult fae to run. I assured them that their material possessions would be restored somehow, that all that mattered was their lives right now.

Two or three fae didn't want to abandon their houses, because that was where they'd raised their children or had last been with their late spouses. My heart ached upon hearing their pleas, seeing the tears in their eyes, but I put on my soldier hat and did what I had to do: I saved my people.

By the time the entire village was taken, we already had everyone marching toward the White City under the moonlight. It was late and everyone was tired, but I needed to get them all very far away from there.

Once they were all gone, I stared at what was left of the village: a pile of black waste under the night sky.

Enraged, I turned to Kei and the captains of my legions. "What the freezing ice happened here?"

Kei lowered his head. "It advanced faster than we expected, my king. When we realized it was going to reach the village in a matter of hours, we started evacuating. The residents of Neige resisted at first. But once they saw the curse coming, they ran away."

I clenched my fists, ready to punch someone, to break something. This couldn't happen. It could *not* happen. But I couldn't blame it all solely on Kei. I should have been here. I should have kept an eye on the curse myself.

Instead, I had been out with Amber, showing her the marketplace, having fun, feeling things I shouldn't feel.

My soul and heart were being pulled in two. I knew I was doing the right thing. What was that human saying? Sacrifice the life of one to save thousands? That was what I was doing here. Then why the frost did it hurt so much? Why did it make me feel sick each time I thought of what I was doing to Amber, the lies I was telling her? I would kill an innocent woman to save my land, my people.

An innocent woman I felt incredibly attracted to.

Today at the marketplace, I had seen Amber smiling wide, laughing, chatting with the fae who probably thought I had claimed her for myself. She had enjoyed tasting different foods and drinks. I had even bought a pair of earrings and given them to her. Why? I had no freezing idea!

Then, at that rooftop, there had been only the two of us. At that moment, there was nothing else I wanted more than to kiss her, than to wrap my arms around her, bring her to me, and have her right there and then.

If Kei hadn't come and interrupted me.... I shook my

head. I didn't know what I would have done. I really didn't want to think about it.

Moreover, I had bigger problems to worry about.

This curse was still advancing, and it seemed to be going faster by the minute. I couldn't just sit here and wait until two weeks passed. There had to be something else I could do now to make this situation better.

Thinking quick, I shifted into my wolf form and took off.

"Cade!" Kei yelled after me.

But I was too fast. I didn't give him a chance to follow me.

I ran alongside the curse until it curved south toward the Tywyll Forest, but it had already taken too much of my land. I ended up at the Triad River, which ran south between the Winter and the Day Courts. Because the curse had poisoned even the banks of the river, at least on the Winter's side, I jumped into the river and let it carry me until it curved right, where the Day Court briefly met with the Tywyll Forest. With my powerful wolf legs, I swam against the current and jumped out of the river.

Right into the Tywyll Forest.

They had cursed my court, turning everything black and dead, but this place was worse. The ground was made of dried, cracked dirt. The scarce trees didn't have any leaves; instead, their branches went so far, they became vines with thousands of thorns. There was no color, no vegetation, no snow, no sand. Just a constant fog over the endless dark desert.

Only Mahaera, Mahaere, and Mahaeru knew how it came to be and how it turned this way, but they had never told anyone.

Knowing the Tabred group wouldn't just curse my court and leave it, I summoned my magic to cloak me and advanced into the forest, close to the riverbank. Using my wolf senses, I sniffed the ground, searching for someone.

A monster.

It didn't take long.

I caught his scent from a mile away and slowly stalked to where he was hiding.

The ugly monster Borak was hiding in the hollow trunk of a dead tree, his deep, dark eyes trained on the horizon, past the river, just watching as the curse advanced and consumed it all.

Breaking my cloaking spell, I lunged at him, closed my jaw on his arm, and dragged him out in the open.

The monster fought against me, his long, slick limbs jerking side to side as he tried to swipe at my head with his claws.

Then I jumped back and shifted into my fae form. Borak started running right away, but I wouldn't let him, not yet. I sent my magic to him. My wind whirled around him, bringing him back to me.

"Let me go!" he cried, jerking against my magic.

I wrapped my wind around him like a mini tornado, keeping him off the ground. There was nothing he could do to get free now.

"Where is Grimmel, that coward?" I asked, barely containing my anger. Borak let out a loud chuckle, but he didn't answer. I focused my wind to close in around him, pressing against him as if he were under the sea. "It was him who sent the curse, wasn't it?"

"It's fun to watch you squirm, King Cadewyn," Borak croaked.

I clenched my fists, willing my magic to be at bay. If it

were up to me, I would squeeze the life out of him right then, but then I wouldn't get what I wanted.

"I have a message for Grimmel," I told him. "Tell him to meet me at the edge of the Tywyll Forest where it meets the Winter and Day Courts tomorrow night. I want to negotiate. Tell him I have an interesting proposition." A lie, since I had nothing to offer him, but I had an entire day to figure something out.

"He'll refuse," Borak said. "Anything you have to offer him, he'll refuse."

"I don't care," I barked. "Just tell him to meet me there." I dropped the magic, and Borak fell to the hard ground. "Go before I change my mind and kill you."

Borak let out a grin. I summoned my magic again, whipping the wind around him and creating ice at his feet.

With wide eyes, Borak turned and ran.

I let out a long breath. Something told me Borak was right. Grimmel would refuse even if I told him I'd give him all of the Winter Court's fortune.

A myriad of emotions created a tornado inside me. I was angry with Grimmel and his people, I was worried about my people and my land, and I was torn about Amber.

I kept forcing myself to believe I was doing the only thing I could do, that I was going to sacrifice the human woman for a greater cause, but those words and those thoughts became heavier and heavier.

With nothing else to do here, I went back to the lost village. Kei grilled me for having disappeared on him, but when I explained to him what I had done, he shut up. Like me, he thought it was a long shot but one I had to try.

"You haven't told her the truth yet, have you?" he asked in

a low voice as we walked with the rest of the village's residents toward the White City.

I shook my head. "Besides you and the three sisters, no one knows the truth."

Kei frowned but didn't say anything. He knew how I felt about lying. I hated it, I hated every second of it, but I didn't see how I could do anything different. If I told her she would have to die for my people, Amber might leave—not that she could leave without me using my medallion to open a portal, but she would try. She would rebel and run—maybe worse, maybe try to take her own life.

My freezing heart squeezed.

A primal instinct hit me square in the chest, making it hard to breathe. There were still hours until we reached the White City with the survivors and helped them settle at a temple or a theater or maybe a school, but I had to go. I had to be there. I had to see her *now*.

"I'll meet you when you arrive at the city," I told Kei before shifting into my wolf form.

I zoomed past my people, my legion, and my knights and raced toward the city—toward the palace. It was full night when I got there, and the palace was already quiet and dark.

Despite it all, I went directly to Amber's room.

The two guards stationed at the door bowed their heads to me.

"Is she inside?" I asked.

"Yes, my king, but she has been asleep for a couple of hours," Niossal told me.

Snow above, I had arrived too late.

Grunting, I marched away from her and into my own chambers, where I took a cold shower to calm me down before I did something stupid. I stayed under the water for a long time, and my body only grew hotter.

I had to do something about this insane need.

The water pouring over my head and back, I splayed a hand on the tile wall in front of me and closed the other around my already hard cock. Just thinking about her, just being near her was enough to make me as hard as steel. A growl started low in my chest as I moved my hand up and down my shaft, imagining her with me—smiling at me, dancing for me, pouting her lips, waiting to be kissed. I grasped my cock harder and moved my hand faster as I imagined pressing her to this wall and sliding inside her. I bet she was tight and wet and warm and—

Snow above, I gritted my teeth as I came, my body shaking as the ecstasy made its way through my system, sending me up to the skies.

Then I came crashing down.

This—Amber and I—couldn't happen. If I ever felt any desire for her again, and I was sure I would, I better just work with my own hand, giving me some kind of release, even if I knew it would never be as good as the real thing.

I stayed under the water for a few minutes, cooling down.

Once I got out and got dressed, I went back into the city and prepared a school to receive the survivors coming this way.

Things were about to get messy.

10

AMBER

I TUGGED the fur coat tighter around me as I walked through the garden. The stone paths weaving alongside the hundreds of leafless, ice-topped trees had been cleared of snow, but the rest of the estate was plain white.

I stopped by a large area where many of the paths met, where a light gray stone fountain stood. The sculpture in the center was of a child fae reaching up with both hands, cupping a crescent moon. There was no water in it, only crystal-clear ice. Even so, the fountain was beautiful, powerful.

Like everything else in this land.

Like the king of this land.

I hadn't seen Cade since he left me at that tower beside the marketplace the day before. Last night, I had asked Tania, one of my handmaids, if she had heard about Cade, but she said he hadn't come back yet.

This wasn't my land, but I was worried about it, and about Cade. He had left so hurriedly after Kei told him about the village. What if something bad had happened to the village? To the village's people? To Cade?

A woman carrying a big wicker basket appeared on the path, startling me. I startled her too, as she gasped and tripped on her own feet, dropping some of the white fruit piling high in the basket.

"I'm sorry, my lady," she said, crouching down to pick them up.

I rushed to her and helped her out. "It was my fault." I picked up one of the fruits. "This is an apple."

"Yes," the woman said with a smile. "A snow apple. They are white and delicious."

I glanced at the woman. The first thing I noticed about her was her brown hair. She clearly wasn't from the Winter Court, but then I noticed something else: she didn't have any pointy ears. She was human like me.

I bit my tongue before I asked her what she was doing here, how she had come here, and why didn't she leave. I frowned, thinking of all the fantasy romance books I had read. In them, faeries kidnapped humans to be their servants, switching them for changelings, and fed them faerie food so they couldn't leave. Was that they case here?

A sick feeling stirred in my stomach. No, it couldn't be. Cade wouldn't do that.

Would he?

I finished picking up the apples and helped the woman up. "Thank you, my lady," she said, bowing her head. "Take one. Try it. You'll like it."

Curious, I picked one of the snow apples, but didn't eat it. I was too wary for that. After another bow of her head, the woman continued down the path toward the castle.

I glanced at the apple in my hand. Human servants, different food, food I wasn't supposed to taste. What if this was a lie too? What if I couldn't eat any of the food in fae land because I too would be trapped here?

Suddenly, I felt very unsure about everything.

I heard the crunch of the snow behind me and thought it was one of the guards who had been following me since I arrived here, coming to tell me I had somewhere to be or even to go back to my bedroom. I understood the palace was a secure place and everyone around here had bodyguards following them around, but sometimes I wondered if they weren't there for my protection but to keep me locked in here.

A figure stood by my side, facing the fountain. His presence, his energy, immediately rubbed against me, and I inhaled deeply.

"Cade," I whispered, turning to face him. He looked at me, and my worry only increased. His hair was messy behind his back, his cloak had dark spots as if he had rubbed against dust or worse, and there were dark circles under his eyes. My fingers itched to touch him. "What happened?"

"We were able to save everyone, but the village was lost to the curse," he said, his voice heavy, tired. "I spent the night settling them in one of the city's schools and making sure they had all they needed."

"I'm sure they are grateful for you," I said, being honest. But then my previous thoughts poked at my mind. "Cade, can I ask you something?"

He didn't hesitate. "Sure."

"Um, it's just...." I glanced at the apple in my hand. "I just saw a human servant carrying a basket full of snow apples."

He furrowed his brow. "You want to know about humans."

"Yes. I mean...I don't know. I guess I'm afraid they are kept here against their will."

"A long time ago, my ancestors kidnapped humans and

brought them here to be our servants. But with time, it changed. The few humans you see working at the castle are descendants of those first servants, but they aren't slaves. They are here because they want to be, and they are treated like any other fae. They receive compensation and vacation." He paused and let out a long sigh. "Though not all kingdoms are like that. Some still bring humans from your world and treat them like slaves."

I believed him. Even though I had no reason, even though he'd brought me here against my will like those slaves many years ago, even though he seemed menacing at times and had no obligation to tell me the truth, I believed him.

"What about this?" I showed him the snow apple. "Can I eat it, or is this one of those foods I shouldn't try?"

One corner of his lips curled up, and my heart skipped a beat. Was that a hint of a smile? "You can eat it," he said. "But let me warn you, it's delicious. You'll want more as soon as you're done with it."

I smiled at him, not sure why.

His blue eyes searched mine, so intent, so deep. My breath caught.

"Cade." We both turned as Kei walked toward us. "Sorry to interrupt, but I need to deliver this to you." He handed Cade a rolled-up paper with a black leather tie.

Frowning, Cade took the paper, unrolled it, and read it. "Snow above," he whispered. Lips pressed into a thin line, Cade nodded once. "Thank you, Kei."

Kei bowed his head to Cade, then to me before whirling on his heels and marching away.

Cade closed his hand tight, crumpling the paper.

"Everything okay?" I knew it wasn't, but I didn't know how to ask him, how to make him talk to me.

"Last night I sent a message to Grimmel, the lead—"

"Leader of the Tabred," I said with a gasp. Why was he reaching out to that monster?

"Yes, you remember." He sounded slightly impressed. "Anyway, I sent him a message asking him to meet me. I wanted to negotiate about the curse, try to convince him to break it himself, to call it back. Anything." He squashed the paper tight in his hands, forming a ball with it. "This was his answer."

"He refused to meet you." From his reaction, it wasn't hard to guess. "But it's okay, right?" I tried smiling again to encourage him. "We still have the ceremony, right? Everything will be okay in the end."

He stared at me, his blue eyes fixed on mine in a way that woke up butterflies in my belly. My cheeks warmed.

"Amber, I would like it if you had dinner with me tonight."

I blinked, stunned. Was this dinner like a date too? I didn't put much thought into it, because if I did, I would become too self-conscious and would act like a hormonal teenager in front of a king.

Despite myself, my smile widened. "I would love to."

I WAS PROBABLY out of my freezing mind for getting close to a woman I would have to kill soon, but I couldn't help myself. Every time I tried staying away, something pulled me to her. Despite all that was going on with my people and my court, I had to check on her, make sure she was okay.

Like a frosting fool, I put on one of my best outfits: white trousers and white tunic with silver embroidery, silver cuffs, and a white leather strap with silver details over my tunic. I also donned my white fur cloak, which I promptly took off when I arrived at the main dining table. The servants had cleaned the room, set the table for two with white plates, silver cutlery, and crystal glasses, and made what was supposed to be delicious fae food with a human twist. Both new and familiar, so Amber could have the best of both worlds.

Chiara entered the dining room a minute after me. She stared at me, deep worry etched on her forehead. "Having dinner with the human?"

Since I hadn't told her why I had brought Amber to the

Winter Court, like all the other fae, except for Kei, she probably thought I was enamored with the human woman. If only it were that simple.

"Just making sure she's comfortable while she's with us," I told my sister.

"Until when will she stay with us?"

I didn't like all these questions. "Why? Wondering if it's worth it to become friends with her?"

Chiara shrugged. "Maybe."

I let out a long sigh. "She'll be gone in less than two weeks. So...don't get attached."

Usually so quiet and aloof but composed, Chiara let me see into her emotions more than ever when her shoulders sagged and her lips turned downward. "I see." She nodded once. "I'll let you enjoy her company alone while you can."

Chiara dragged her feet out of the dining room, and I felt like a freezing bastard. For the first time in forever, my sister had shown interest in something other than just herself and her own world, and I was going to take that away from her.

I could have at least invited her to stay for dinner with us, but at the moment, I didn't feel like sharing Amber with anyone.

I was glad I hadn't called Chiara back when Amber arrived a few minutes later.

She stepped into the dining room and my breath caught.

Her long, dark hair was pulled into an intricate braid at the back of her head, with half of it curled down over her shoulder. Her makeup was delicate but perfect for her beautiful face. And her dress...it was a simple, strapless, silver gown that hugged her full breasts, tiny waist, and hips perfectly. The skirt flared out past her hips, reminding me of the movement of the wind when she walked up to me.

With a barely contained smile, she spun in front of me, showing off how stunning she was.

"Sorry," she said, forcing her smile away. "It's just...I've never worn anything like this. I feel like I'm a princess in a fairy tale."

"You look beautiful," I said, unable to take my eyes off her.

"Thanks," she whispered. A faint pink shade spread through her cheeks.

Something shone from her ears, and I noticed she was wearing the snowflake earrings I had given to her. I didn't know why, but I was glad she put them on. "I see you like the earrings."

She touched her ears, her cheeks turning redder. "I love them."

My fingers itched to reach out and touch her again, to run my fingers over her blush, down her long neck, around her shoulder, and—

I shook my head once, trying to rein in those thoughts. I had already established it wasn't worth it to get close to her, to let her charm me.... Who was I kidding? I was so freezing charmed right then.

I guided her to the table and pulled out her chair so she could sit down. Then I took my place at the head of the table. Servants came in to bring us drinks and appetizers. When selecting the menu, I also talked to Gauri, the head of the staff, to make sure to keep humans away from the dining room. I had been honest with Amber when I told her that the humans who worked here were all treated the same as the fae. They were here because they wanted to be. But I didn't want to risk having her doubting me, not tonight.

When we were left alone again, I asked her, "Is your stay here comfortable? Is there anything I can do for you?"

She fixed those green eyes on mine. "This place is magical, and everything is great." A small smile stretched over her lips. "Thank you for caring."

I frowned. I cared, didn't I? Too frosting much, actually. That was quite alarming. I rummaged through my mind, trying to think of a subject to talk about that wouldn't remind me of how beautiful she was and how badly I wanted to have her, but it was Amber who spoke first.

"If you don't mind, I would like to know more about you."

My frown deepened. "What do you mean?"

She shrugged, reaching for her crystal goblet full of white wine. "Besides the war with the Tabred clan from Tywyll Forest and your sister Chiara, I know nothing about you or your kingdom. Or the entire fae realm, actually."

I inhaled, putting myself in her shoes. The first time I went to the human world, I also didn't know anything and asked a million questions. "Let's see. We're in Wyth, that's the name of this continent in the fae realm, and there are eight courts in Wyth: Winter, Spring, Summer, Autumn, Dawn, Day, Dusk, and Night."

"Are there more courts or continents?"

I nodded. "There is a desert island to the north and more continents, but they are too far away. We never travel there or receive any news from them."

"So, the eight courts are sort of alone."

"In a way, yes. You know that to the south there is the Tywyll Forest, but it isn't considered a part of Wyth. The only interaction we have with them is to keep them back from invading our courts."

"You're at war with the Tabred clan," she said. "Are there other groups, and are they at war with other courts?"

"Only the Day Court borders with the Tywyll Forest

besides us, and they have a similar situation as we do. They are at war with another clan, but the war has been dormant for a few years now. Hopefully, they won't end up like us anytime soon."

Amber let go of her wine and rested her hand over mine. "I'm sorry."

A pang cut through my heart. I stared at her hand, so soft and warm over mine, then looked at her bright eyes. "For?"

"The curse, fighting for your land, the war." She paused. "Losing your father."

"I lost my mother in the war too," I told her, surprising even myself with those words. Her eyes widened. "She was a warrior, always had been. After falling in love, becoming mates, and marrying, my father tried to control her and keep her from the army, but being just a queen wasn't for her. She needed to be in the middle of the chaos, coordinating the battlefield. When I was little, the Tabred clan invaded us, not from the south but the west, using the Triad River as their path. We weren't prepared, but she went there with her main legion and pushed them back. Though, she lost her life in doing so. Losing her drove my father into a deep depression. Chiara and I were young, but we had to step up and help out with the court's ruling whenever we could. I think our enemies noticed our court was unbalanced and our leader was weakened. That was when they struck and killed my father too."

"I'm so sorry." She squeezed my hand. "How old were you?"

"Young by our standard but not too young for you."

She tilted her head to the side. "What does that mean?"

"Fae age slower than humans. Though I heard human fantasy books say we are immortal, that isn't true. We live up to eight hundred years old, sometimes even a thousand years."

"Hm, how old are you?"

I suppressed a smile. I hadn't smiled in so many years, I had forgotten how, but now with Amber around me, I was learning to again. However, it was still hard for me to let it out. "In human years? I'm twenty-eight. In fae? I'm two hundred and twenty-four."

Amber froze. "Wow. That's... interesting." She brought her goblet to her lips and drank a long swallow. Her shock was amusing, and I felt myself wanting to smile again. "Tell me what else you can do. I mean, I know you can conjure ice and wind. Can all Winter Court fae do that?"

"Conjuring ice, snow, and frost, and manipulating the wind are all Winter Court fae traits, but not all of them can do it all," I told her. "Some can conjure snow but not ice. Some can only manipulate the wind." I turned my free hand and summoned my power. A small ball of ice appeared in my palm. "But those aren't all." I deposited the ball of ice in an empty glass. "Compared to humans, fae are faster, more agile, have increased hearing and sight." Which explained why sometimes, when there were only the two of us, I could hear the rapid beating of her heart. Like now. "And I can also shift into a frost wolf."

Her mouth opened. "Are you serious?"

I nodded. "Again, not all Winter Court fae can do it, but most of the higher fae can."

"That sounds very cool." She pouted her lips, thinking. "I think that if I could shift into an animal, I would choose a black panther."

"Why?" I asked, genuinely curious.

Amber shrugged. "I don't know. I just think they look pretty and are very fierce and strong."

Just like her.

A moment later, a servant walked in the dining room, bringing the first course of our dinner. Instantly, Amber pulled her hand from mine, as if I had burned her.

I understood why she did it, because she thought we couldn't be seen like that. The truth was, we probably shouldn't be, but who were we fooling here? For days now I had been all over her and not hiding it. By now rumors that the king had found his mate had probably spread far and wide.

If only it was that simple.

AFTER DINNER, I invited Amber to walk through the castle with me. I showed her the handful of winter rooms we had at the corners of the castle: large rooms with ice-like glass walls and ceilings, where sometimes I hosted a party or two. During the night, the north one was the best since the moon could be seen from the glass windows. High in the sky, the blue moon illuminated the interior, reflecting off the white stone floor, giving the place an eerie shine. Amber didn't want to leave the winter room, but I told her I had some other place to show her.

I took her to the courtyard in the center of the palace.

"What is this place?" she asked as we walked out. The air was chilly, and Amber immediately hugged herself. I wondered if her coat was enough for her in this cold.

She didn't seem bothered by the cold, though, as she glanced side to side, her eyes round. Even though it was late night, the moon reflected off the white stones of the palace wall, illuminating the entire courtyard with a faint blue glow.

"This was just a simple courtyard before, with benches and some bushes."

"And snow, I bet."

"And snow, of course." I fought off a grin. "But once my father found my mother and learned she was his mate, he made this for her." I spread my hands wide. We walked slowly by a snow-cleared stone path, weaving through waist-height ice sculptures. The path ended in the center of the courtyard, where there was a small ice gazebo. Underneath the gazebo, there was no snow, but plenty of midnight iris. "My mother's favorite flowers."

"How?" Amber asked, approaching the flowers. She leaned forward and ran her fingertips over a velvety, dark-blue petal. "I assumed flowers didn't bloom in the Winter Court."

"They don't," I told her. "But my father paid handsomely to have a witch come and spell the ground."

Amber's back snapped straight. "Witches? You mean, witches exist?"

I nodded. "Why? Did you think fae were the only other beings besides humans?"

"I just...I never considered this. Until a few days ago, I didn't even know about fae." She narrowed her eyes. "So, if witches exist, then what else is out there?"

"Vampires, werewolves, demons, mermaids...take your pick."

"Wow." She stared at the flowers again. "It'll be hard going back to my boring life after knowing all of this."

I stared at her, at the faint moonlight dancing over her silky skin, her luscious hair. Why in the frost was I doing this?

Why was I torturing her, and myself, like this? She would never go back to her boring life because I was going to kill her soon.

I had to kill her.

My heart squeezed, and my breath caught.

I didn't want to kill her.

Letting my desire speak louder, I reached down and plucked a flower from the ground. Slowly, I turned to Amber and placed the flower behind her ear. She stared at me, her eyes searching mine, her breathing shallow.

I couldn't resist her.

I didn't want to resist her.

Too far gone, I looked at her parted lips and leaned into her. I moved slowly, giving her time to pull away if she didn't want this. But she didn't pull away. Instead, she stretched her neck, getting closer to me.

Snow above....

I inhale deeply, taking in her intoxicating flowery scent. With a growl, I brushed my lips against hers. One more chance for her to pull back. Just one more.

She didn't.

I closed my mouth over hers, claiming her lips, claiming her tongue, claiming her soul. Right at that moment, I didn't care about fated mates, commitments, and whatnots. All I cared about was tasting her, having her.

With a whimper, Amber opened up for me, letting me in. I teased her tongue with mine, exploring her mouth, drinking her in. I wrapped my hand around her waist and pulled her to me. Her body melted against mine, the soft curves of her breasts pressed tight against my chest.

As the crown prince and later king of the Winter Court, I couldn't—shouldn't—be seen around with any female. I was supposed to wait for my mate, but there had been times when I had been weak. There was only so much I could resist.

But I had never felt so weak, so defeated, as I felt with Amber.

This pure-hearted, selfless human could not have any real magic and power of her own, but she sure as frost had some power over me.

Her hands traveled up and around my neck until she buried them under my hair at my nape, tugging slightly.

A rush of heat coursed through me.

Snow above....

I deepened the kiss, my hands slowly trekking up her back to find the buttons of her dress. I needed to get her naked. I needed to take her. I had to have her. Right here, right now. My fingertips trailed the skin on her back right above the dress, and Amber moaned against my mouth.

The little sound sent a wave of heat to my hips, making me crazy.

Really crazy.

This was more than crazy; it was insane.

I jumped back, putting well over four feet between Amber and me. Off balance, Amber almost fell to the ground. I reached for her but stopped myself.

This was truly insane. I had to keep telling myself that; otherwise I would give in again. Especially when she looked up at me, confused. But the confusion was quickly gone. A glint of anger fell over her green eyes, and she hugged herself.

"I'm sorry," I forced myself to say. "I shouldn't have done that."

"If you say so," she whispered.

Those words, her voice...they cut through my chest, and I had to fight against myself not to reach for her again. She didn't know her future; how could she understand why I was so desperately trying to stay the frost away?

"I'll send someone to escort you back to your room."

Feeling like the biggest bastard on Wyth, I spun around and marched away.

It was all I could do before I actually went through with my desire, with my want, and made everything worse.

I EXITED the Moon Temple after another cleansing session, hugging my coat tight, and walked the path back to the palace, the guard who had been assigned to me following me. The weather was just as cold and gloomy as before, but for some reason it bothered me more now.

For some reason? Who was I trying to fool? I knew the reason why my mood had been so blue in the past three days. Because Cade had kissed me as if his life depended solely on my lips, and out of nowhere, he broke it off and left me alone in the cold.

Apparently kissing me was terrible, since I hadn't seen or heard from him in three days. I had walked around the palace and the gardens all day long, hoping I would bump into him, but soon I learned he wasn't in the palace at all.

I felt guilty, dirty, disappointed. That had been the second time he rejected me loud and clear. The first had been a mishap on my part, when I thought I was dreaming about him and this place, but the second time.... I had thought he wanted it; after all, he was the one who started it. He was the one who shoved his tongue down my throat and awoke a hunger in my body I didn't even know I had. Watching steamy videos and reading steamy books would never compare to what I felt when he claimed my lips, when he pulled me against him, when he touched my skin.

But then he hadn't just left me alone in the courtyard. He had left the palace and hadn't come back in three freaking days.

Frustrated, I halted in the middle of the path and stomped my foot.

"Anything wrong, my lady?" Niossal, my guard, asked.

"No, no," I said with a long breath. "It's all fine." A lie, but what would I say to him? That I was mad at his king for making me all hot and bothered and not finishing what he had started?

But at the same time, I understood Cade. As an honorable king, he was waiting for his mate to appear. He had said a couple of times that he shouldn't fool around; otherwise he wouldn't be taken as a serious and committed king. His people were waiting for their queen, probably more than Cade was waiting for his mate.

I was just in the way. Even if Cade had thought about sleeping with me, even if only for a minute, he'd probably come to the conclusion it wasn't worth it.

One day he would find the one and live happily after ever.

Holy shit, my mood was even worse now. I needed to find something to do to occupy my mind, something that would take a long time, something I liked, something—

I knew what to do!

With renewed purpose, I entered the palace, turned to the back rooms, and went to the underground level. At the stairs,

Niossal caught up with me. "My lady, you shouldn't be here. Let me escort you to your room."

"Shush," I told him, though I had a smile on my lips.

The first room on the underground level was the kitchen —a large, wide place with lots of cabinets, counters, and islands. The fae working there all stopped what they were doing and looked at me.

"My lady, what are you doing here?" Tania asked. "Are you hungry? I can take something to you in your bedroom."

I shook my head. "I'm not hungry. I want to help."

She stared at me with huge eyes. "What?"

"In the human world, I worked at a restaurant," I told her. Then I turned to the head cook, Merry. I had seen her before, learned her name, but never spoke to her. "I didn't cook there, but it's one of my passions. Let me help you."

Merry shook her head vehemently. "If King Cadewyn finds out I let you in here, he'll have my head." The plump fae trudged forward and pushed me back. "You better go."

"I'm not going," I said, my words firm. I was damn tired of being told where to go and what to do. I still had ten days in this land. I would go insane if I didn't do something. "Just go on about your day, and I'll work by myself, as quiet and out of the way as I can."

I sidestepped her and looked around the kitchen, trying to find a corner where I could work without bothering them. Ignoring the stares and whispers, I settled at the corner of an island right in the middle of the kitchen. Then I tried familiarizing myself with it. To the left, there was a giant pantry with many refrigerators—though they looked five hundred years older than anything I had seen on Earth. To the right were the cabinets with pots, pans, bowls, utensils, and more. Each island, or station, was equipped with a stove, range, and sink. There was no microwave, but I wasn't planning on using one.

First, I went to the pantry and looked over the ingredients. There were plenty of things I had no idea what they were, but all that I needed to make my favorite treat was right there. I picked the ingredients and took them to my station. Then I went to the cabinets and grabbed the pans and pots I would need.

When I came back to my station, Tania showed up beside me. She had a folded cloth in her hand. "Here. Since I can't convince you to leave, then at least wear these."

I took them from her, and even before I could see them and thank her, she was gone. I unfolded the cloth; it was an apron and a bandana. With a smile, I wrapped the apron around me and used the bandana to tie my hair back.

Then I got to work.

The fae kept stealing glances at me, probably wondering what I was doing. When my treat was in the oven and the delicious aroma began to fill the kitchen, they started commenting on how nice it smelled. Since the oven here was also outdated, I kept a close eye on my treat, afraid I would burn it.

When the first baking sheet was out of the oven and cooling on my station's corner, Merry came over to me.

"What's that?" she asked, eyeing the baking sheet with suspicion.

I cut a small square and offered it to her. "It's hazelnut chocolate brownie with almond pieces."

She took the piece of brownie from me, sniffed it, then shoved it into her mouth. Her eyes bugged. "Snow above, this is delicious."

I smiled wide. "Glad you say that, because I made *a lot*." I pulled out the other two baking sheets from the oven. "These two are for all of you."

The fae gathered around my station. I cut squares off the brownie and put them on plates before passing them around. In no time, all the fae were smiling at me, thanking me for the treat, and asking me if they could help me with anything else.

"Actually, I want a favor from the head of staff." I turned to Gauri, who had showed up a few minutes ago and had instantly reprimanded me for being there. Tania had given me a square of fabric, where I put as many slices of brownie as I could, then knotted the edges of the fabric, forming a small package. "I want to send this to the king, wherever he is."

She eyed me with suspicion again, but she took the bundle from me. "I heard one of the soldiers is going to meet with the king later this afternoon. I can send this with him."

I felt relieved. "Thank you."

She shook her head but left the kitchen, and I assumed she was going to find this soldier.

Feeling lighter and better, I turned to my station. Some fae still stole pieces of brownie, but most had gone back to work. Happy to be doing something, I cleaned up my mess, even though two fae complained that was their job, and started cooking something else.

CADE

COWARD, that was what I was.

For three days, I had been a coward and hidden away from the White Palace. Every cell in my body screamed for me to go back and finish what Amber and I started that night, but it wasn't right. I couldn't take advantage of her now and later sacrifice her to save my court.

So I kept myself busy. First, I checked on the fae lodging at the school in the White City. I brought extra clothes, food, and toys for the kids. But it wasn't enough. They couldn't stay in the school forever. If we didn't break this curse soon, I wasn't sure what would happen to them.

Then, I went to check on the curse. It was advancing, inch by inch, and soon would overtake another one of my villages. So I called on Kei and the biggest of my legions so we could start evacuating the residents sooner rather than later. We worked relentlessly for over thirty hours, trying to convince my people to move, then helping them pack essentials and sending them north on the main road, toward the White City, where I would have to find another place to house more of the refugees.

We had more time with this village, but still some fae, especially the older ones, were adamant about not going. I could simply carry them out, but I tried reasoning with them first. They had to understand what was going on. They had to obey their king.

On the afternoon of my third day away from the palace, Kei rode around the village, checking for the curse's advancement. Meanwhile, the six White Knights and I went around the village, entering the houses and making sure no one was left behind.

We stopped by the center square in the village to rest.

"I don't trust staying here, my king," Xitan, one of the White Knights, said. "We should leave."

"Kei will be back soon." I took a long sip of water. "If the curse was already here, he would have told us."

Xitan didn't seem convinced. He kept glancing around with worry etched on his forehead. Well, all my White Knights seemed worried.

I was worried too, but the curse wasn't that fast. Besides, we had already evacuated the entire village, I was sure. We were just going around one more time for my peace of mind.

The sound of a horse trotting made me stand up. It was a young soldier, the one who brought me important messages from the castle every day.

He stopped the horse, jumped down, and bowed his head to me. "Greetings, my king."

"Any news?" I asked, noticing he was holding a folded cloth in his hands.

"Nothing new, my king," the young soldier said. "The refugees are becoming agitated but remain contained.

Mahaeru showed up there while I was checking on them and receiving the reports. She said she'd talk to the theater and see if they can schedule some free showings for the refugees, just to give them something to do."

"That's a good idea," I said, surprised by the goddess. I expected that of one of her sisters, not from Mahaeru herself. "We should find more activities like that, especially for the kids."

"I'll start a list," the young soldier said. "Oh, this was sent to you, my king." He extended his arms, offering me the folded cloth.

I took it from him, realizing there was something inside. "What is this?"

"Gauri asked me to bring this to you," the soldier said. "There's a note inside."

I unfolded the flaps of the cloth and found something that looked like chocolate cake, but smelled even better, and a small note.

I picked up the note and read it.

My dear king,

Today I learned your human knows how to cook like one of those angels humans believe in. However, Merry asked me to tell you she doesn't like strangers in her kitchen. Please, come get your human.

Gauri

I frowned. This was sent by Amber? To me? I gave it to Xitan. "You all can share this."

Determined to not fall for her charms, I turned away from them and the scent of that cake.

The White Knights didn't waste any time. Tired and working nonstop because of me, they were probably also hungry since I had barely stopped to eat anything.

I heard gasps and moans from my fierce, strong knights.

"My king, this is delicious," Xitan said. "I think you should at least try it before it's all gone."

I crossed my arms, trying to contain myself. I had to be strong and honorable and resist temptations. That was what a king was. Someone who had to make hard choices, who stuck to the right path, who endured the unimaginable for his court, who abdicated his own well-being for his people.

But when Xitan got closer, bringing that sweet scent back to my nose, I gave in. I reached into the cloth and picked up a small square of gooey chocolate cake.

I bit into it.

Sweet, warm flavors I had never experienced before, not together, exploded in my mouth, and I suddenly wished I hadn't shared it with the knights and had eaten the whole thing by myself.

This cake thing was delicious, almost as much as Amber was. And now I was craving her again.

A desire to run back to the White Palace hit me hard, making me breathless. I needed to see her. I need to talk to her. I needed to hold her against me, to kiss her, to have her.

All of her.

Almost mindlessly, I took a step forward.

"Run!" Kei's shout pierced through my skull. The knights and I turned toward it. Galloping through the streets, Kei urged his horse to go faster. "Run!" he shouted again. "The curse is here! It's coming fast!"

My stomach dropped.

The knights flanked me, and along with the young soldier, we ran up the main street toward the edge of the village.

Just then, we heard something else.

"Help!"

My knees locked. I halted and glanced around. "Did you hear it?"

"Yes," Xitan said.

Kei brought his horse to a stop beside us. "There's no time." He jumped off and pushed me to the horse. "Just go."

"Help! We're here!" we heard again.

"Fan out and find them!" I shouted to my knights.

"No!" Kei said, his tone defiant. I could count on the fingers of one hand how many times Kei had defied me like that, especially in front of others. "Look!" He pointed back.

The curse, black and thick and relentless, advanced through the village like an ocean wave, faster than I had ever seen it. Streets, houses, fences, pillars... everything crumbled underneath it, becoming pure darkness.

"Help us, please!"

I glanced around, my heart beating fast against my chest, bringing on too much pain, too much despair. Finally, I found them. A couple of elders behind a glass window on the second floor of a small house on the other side of the square.

Just inches away from being taken by the darkness.

I ran to them, but Kei and Xitan held my arms, pulling me back. "We have to save them."

The elders punched on the glass. They tried to open the window, but it wouldn't budge. I remembered seeing them before, early this morning. They had been very upset when I told them we needed to evacuate the village. They had been two of the many who said they wouldn't go anywhere. But I had convinced them to join the rest and march away.

Or at least I thought I had.

They must have come back later, when my legion and I were busy, and slipped into their house undetected. I didn't know why they did that. Did they think we were bluffing? That we were going through this freezing craziness because it was fun? Perhaps they thought they would be safe on the second floor, or that the curse wouldn't advance as fast, or that it would stop somehow. I didn't know, and I didn't care.

All I cared about was that they were seeing the curse coming for them, they wanted out, and I wanted to save them.

"It's too late," Kei said, his voice breaking.

With renewed force, the curse became an avalanche, and in less than three seconds swallowed the house whole.

I stilled, my eyes wide, my mind blank.

No, this couldn't be happening.

"Let's go, my king," Xitan begged. "We need to go. Now!"

Kei tugged on my arm, and I awoke from this nightmare. If I didn't go, Kei, the White Knights, and the young soldiers would stay with me. We would all die, and we wouldn't be able to help other people.

We needed to go.

I shoved the young soldier on the horse. "Go fast. Tell the others to speed up and march away."

"But what about you, my king?" the young soldier asked, his face pale.

"We'll be right behind you." I slapped the horse's side, and it took off. "As for us, we shift into our wolves and we outrun this freezing curse."

Kei and my knights dipped their chins once, letting me know they were ready when I was. I quickly shifted into my wolf form, and they did the same.

Then we ran out of the village together.

A safe distance from the village, we stopped and watched. Once everything was gone, the curse slowed down to its regular pace. Somehow this curse was spelled so it took over towns in a matter of minutes, not giving us much time to save anyone.

We can't risk this happening again, I said into Kei's mind. *We need to evacuate all villages in the curse's path, or close to it. I won't lose anyone else.*

If you allow me, I'll go to Winterlis right now and start, he said.

Winterlis. That was the next village in the curse's path. *Please do.*

He took off.

And I watched the village, now gone under the darkness.

For a moment there, I had almost succumbed to my desire and gone after Amber. This tragedy sobered me. It was clear I couldn't let my lust speak louder. I couldn't risk falling for Amber, because if I fell for her, I wouldn't be able to kill her, and I had to. If I wanted to stop this frosting curse and save my people, I had to sacrifice her.

With that in mind, I decided to keep working with my legion to move my people, evacuate villages, make sure they were well accommodated in the White City, and stay away from the White Palace until it was time for the sacrifice.

That was the only way this would work.

14

AMBER

AFTER MY SUCCESSFUL batches of hazelnut chocolate brownie, I had been welcomed at the kitchen. In the last two days, I had been there three times. By now, the staff of the palace all waited with bated breath for my next dish, even when it was something as simple as French toast or a cheese omelet.

But I didn't want to spend my afternoons solely at the kitchen, so I had my guards show me the library.

When I first stepped foot inside the library, I thought I had found paradise. It was an enormous room with triple ceiling height, long and narrow windows, too many shelves, and even more books. In the middle, there were two long, white tables with many comfortable armchairs, and two white velvet couches.

My first time there, I went around checking out what kinds of books a fae library could hold. I was amused to find some classics from the human world, like books by Tolstoy, Jane Austen, and even J.R.R. Tolkien. There were encyclopedias and books about bigger countries, like the United States, Russia, and Australia, all showing maps, relating facts about culture, and telling a little about the history.

Then there were the fae books. There was a fiction section and a nonfiction. It seemed they wrote fiction books just like humans. There were romance, sci-fi, fantasy, mystery, suspense, thriller, and horror. And the nonfiction were about their magic, their history, their culture, and more.

Since I didn't know much about their world, I started with those. I picked a few books about Wyth's history and sat down on the couch, where I started skimming through them all.

In the few hours I spent here every day, I skimmed through at least a dozen books and learned a lot of things. I saw a map of Wyth with the eight courts, a small inaccessible area in the center called Niwtrall, Tywyll Forest at the south, and the unnamed desert island to the north. Wyth was several thousands of years old, and the continent's land was supposedly alive and magical. Niwtrall was actually some kind of core, from where all the magic in Wyth came, turning that small piece of land into the most powerful being in all Wyth.

I learned that Mahaera, the fae who conducted my cleansing rituals, was a goddess and that she had two sisters, Mahaere and Mahaeru, each one with a different personality. They had been here since the beginning of the world, but no one knew exactly how they had come to be and what exactly they did for the world, other than show up and help here and there. Another interesting fact about them was that even though there were three of them, nobody had ever seen them together.

I read about higher and lesser fae, terms I had heard before from Cade and the others but felt bad about asking, as if it was a personal question they didn't want to answer. Higher fae were royals and nobles, fae who came from stronger families and thus had more magic. Lesser fae were the town workers, the castle's staff and servants, fae with little or no magic. The book also detailed that even though fae had long lives and were very resilient, they weren't immortal. They could die from a severe illness, a bad wound, or a direct hit to the heart, just like humans.

One entire book I skimmed was about the fae traits and magic. Changelings were true, but like Cade said, the Winter Court didn't work like that anymore. The sight, which I had been given by Cade, was a spell capable of making humans see fae glamour and most of their magic. The speech, also a gift from Cade, was a spell that could make anyone speak the fae language. The stuff about food was true. Some of it was like strong drugs to humans, some drove us mad, some even killed us instantly, but no food could trap us here, like I had read in some fantasy romance novels before. Another thing I remembered from novels was that iron was like poison to fae. That was true too. Also, fae mated for life. Like Cade had told me, not all fae found their mates, but those who did spent the rest of their lives with their mates. If a fae's mate died, they didn't find another. It was a once-in-a-lifetime thing. Also, the mating call acted differently for each fae. Some could smell their mates from afar and find them like that. Others had to be intimate with their mate for the bond to snap. This mate thing was either romantic or not. If I was fae, would I like to find the one for me? What if I didn't like him? That was nonsense I didn't have to worry about.

In the next book, I learned about the government of each court. A few facts stuck in my mind, like the fact that the Summer Court currently had only a queen, named Natsia, which was uncommon for Wyth. Usually, males rose to be king, then married their mates and made them queens. Queens were rare but not unheard of. The Dusk Court was quiet and reclusive, rarely attending special events or meetings from other courts. And the Night Court had the only high fae twin set in the whole of Wyth: Prince Nox and Princess Amaya, who were said to be selfish and spoiled. Last but not least, the Spring Court had had a civil war that started thirty years ago and lasted for over fifteen years. The current king had killed his older brother and the entire royal family, leaving only himself to take the throne.

I also learned that over a thousand years ago, five of the eight courts were at war for reasons no one seemed to understand. The war lasted for about a hundred years—called the Hundred Year War—and decimated almost half their populations. After that, all eight courts signed a peace treaty, which remained in effect. Sometimes the alliances and friendships were tested, but since then, the eight courts hadn't fought against each other.

I also learned that Cade—or Cadewyn—had been crowned king ninety-three years ago, when he was only one hundred and thirty-one, making him one of the youngest kings ever crowned in Wyth.

Sometimes, Chiara would show up at the library and explain to me about the things I was reading about.

"The medallions are magical objects," she said, seated by my side and pointing to the picture of the medallion in the book in front of me. "They were forged at Niwtrall, and their sole purpose is to open portals to other worlds."

I frowned. "That was how Cade went to the human world and brought me here."

She nodded. "Yes. And when he takes you back once the ceremony is done, he'll use it again."

My heart squeezed at the thought of going back to Earth. Maybe it was silly of me, but right now, I was liking the Winter Court more and more, and every time I remembered how my life was in shambles back home, it made me anxious. I wasn't sure I wanted to go back to that mess.

The next day, Chiara stopped by the library to let me know she had appointments in the White City and wouldn't be back until later. I felt touched that she bothered to tell me that at all. Cade had mentioned she was reserved, and even though her movements were stoic and some of her comments were too direct, she was nice to me and I was warming up to her.

After she left, I sank into the couch and continued reading and learning more about Wyth and fae in general. I was reading about the different kinds of magic in Wyth when some odd sounds caught my attention. I frowned, noticing it was coming from outside. Curious, I went to the window and spied out. A yellowish-brown carriage approached the main gates, followed by several soldiers on light brown horses.

"Light brown?" I muttered to myself, trying to think of the books I had just read. One of them had specified the colors of each court.

"It's the Spring Court," Niossal said from behind me, his eyes on the window.

We watched as the carriage stopped in front of the palace's main staircase and an elegant male fae stepped out, his short blond hair combed back.

"Who's that?" I asked. A few days ago, Niossal had been cold and quiet. But after I gave him a slice of hazelnut chocolate brownie, he had loosened up a little. He was still quiet, but at least he wasn't cold anymore.

"King Vasant," Niossal said, his voice tight. "What is he doing here? King Cadewyn didn't tell us about any court visiting."

"Is that a problem?" I asked, curious. Everything about this place made me curious. I frowned, remembering what I had just learned. Spring Court. Was this the king who had killed his own brother for the throne?

"King Cadewyn doesn't like him." Niossal turned to me. "My lady, please stay here. I'll check what's going on and be right back."

I nodded. "All right."

After a slight bow, Niossal left, but not before saying something to the other guard. I returned my attention to the view beyond the window. But then King Vasant was escorted inside the palace, and despite the absurd number of foreign soldiers in the palace's front garden, everything seemed to go back to normal.

This visit certainly didn't concern me, so I went back to the couch and continued reading for the next hour. I had barely noticed the time passing, but then Tania entered the library, saying it was time for supper.

I followed her through the palace hallways, just now realizing Niossal hadn't come back yet. A sliver of worry snaked through me. Was something wrong?

I opened my mouth to ask Tania if she knew anything, but someone new stepped in the hallway.

"King Vasant," Tania whispered, lowering her head.

I frowned, my eyes on the Spring king. I hadn't bowed to Cade once since I arrived here; I wouldn't start doing that for another king, especially not one who had murdered his own family.

With a lopsided grin, Vasant walked toward me. "What do we have here? A human in the Winter Court?" He glanced around. "I heard rumors about you. You're Cadewyn's new pet." What did he mean, new pet? The way he said it made me think Cade had had more *pets*. "Hm, you're with a hand-maid and a guard. You must be a special pet. What's your name?"

Vasant was a tall male fae, but not as wide as Cade. He wore a beautiful dark-green armor with golden embroidery and a heavy golden crown atop his head. He also had a long, golden sword resting at his waist. His dark-blue eyes shone with mischief, and that nasty grin only widened. This king smelled of arrogance and selfishness. Even if I didn't know he was a murderer, that would have been enough to make me dislike him.

I lifted my chin. "I don't think that concerns you."

Vasant tsked. "Don't you know who I am, little human?"

Tania tugged at the skirt of my dress. "He's a king, my lady. Please, bow to him and answer his questions."

"See?" Vasant gestured to Tania. "Your handmaid knows how you should behave. You better listen to her."

I gritted my teeth. Usually, I tried seeing the best in every person, even the ones who committed crimes. But there were criminals who couldn't be forgiven and didn't deserve pity or consideration. For some reason, Vasant reminded me of these criminals. The more I stood before him, the more he rubbed me the wrong way.

For Cade's sake, I forced a curtsy. "If you'll excuse me, I have somewhere to be."

I started walking again, but Tania and my guard didn't

move. King Vasant took a step to the side, blocking my way. "Cadewyn's servants are preparing a feast for me. Why don't you join me?"

"I don't think—"

He closed the distance between us, his teeth gritted. He loomed over me, and I resisted the temptation of stepping back. I wouldn't show him that he was frightening me. "I'm not asking, little pet." He closed his hand around my wrist and pulled me with him.

"Let me go!" I protested, trying to pry his fingers from my wrist but to no avail. Before I knew it, we were in the dining room, the same one where I'd had dinner with Cade five nights ago.

"Sit here," he said, pushing me down in a chair at the dining table.

I immediately started to stand up. "I won't—" Vines shot up from the stone floor and entwined around my legs and arms, tying me to the chair. "What the hell are you doing?"

Vasant turned his dark-blue eyes to me. "Little pet, let me teach you one thing: I'm a king, and you're a bug. You'll do what I say. If you don't, it'll only make things harder."

I gulped. "What will be harder?"

The wicked grin was back on his lips, but he didn't say anything.

Finally, Tania and my guard entered the dining room.

"King Vasant, I ask you to let Lady Amber go, please," Tania said, looking at her feet.

"Hm, Amber," Vasant mused. "That's your name?"

"Please, King Vasant," Tania insisted.

Vasant lifted his hand into the air, and vines sprouted from the floor and quickly wrapped around Tania's neck, choking her. Tania fell to her knees, clawing at the vines.

"Stop this!" I yelled. "You're hurting her!"

Vasant shrugged. "Isn't that the point?"

My guard knelt on the floor, his head bowed. "Please, King Vasant, let Lady Amber and the handmaid go."

Without mercy, Vasant spun around, drawing his sword and pointing to the guard's nose. "Interrupt me again, and I'll kill the handmaid and cut Lady Amber up in small pieces and send them to King Cadewyn in a gift box." He swung the sword, bringing its point to my neck. I gasped. "Now, be a good boy and ask your cook to send me the best fae wine in the cellar, along with some appetizers. I was promised a feast."

The guard hesitated, but in the end, he lowered his head and rushed toward the kitchen.

I jerked against the vines, but they only tightened around my arms and legs, digging into my skin.

"Stop fighting, or it'll be worse, my little pet," Vasant warned.

"I'll stop fighting if you let the handmaid go," I proposed, stilling my body.

Instantly, the vines around Tania's neck loosened. She scurried out of the dining room, probably afraid that Vasant would change his mind and use her again. I couldn't blame her.

Once we were alone again, Vasant took the chair beside me and leaned closer. "You're beautiful, did you know that? For a human, you're gorgeous. I can see why Cadewyn wanted to play with you."

I wanted to defend Cade's honor, and mine too, and say it wasn't like that, but I wouldn't waste my breath with this ruthless, pretentious king. With a personality like that, did he care for his court as much as Cade cared for his? I seriously doubted it.

A male fae servant came into the room carrying a large tray with a wine bottle, two goblets, and a bowl with some kind of chips. He didn't glance my way as he set the tray on the table and said, "The feast is almost ready, King Vasant. Please, enjoy this treat until then." Folding his middle even more, the fae backed away until he disappeared from the room.

I wanted to shout for help, any help, but I had already concluded with Vasant's threat and the way he had hurt Tania, no one would come. No one could come, even if they wanted to.

I bet they were all just as disgusted with Vasant's behavior as I was. What a king he was....

Vasant took the wine bottle, uncorked it, and sniffed. "Hm, this is the good wine." He poured a little of the drink in each goblet. "My little pet, have you tasted fae wine before? Do you know what it does to humans?"

My brows slanted down. "I know what it does."

His lopsided grin was back. "From your answer, I'll assume you haven't tasted it." He reached for a goblet, took a long swallow, then grabbed the bottle again. "Here. I'll show you."

He stood and reached for me.

"What are you doing?" I asked, panic stamped in my voice.

"I'm showing you a good time," he said, tangling his hand in my long hair. "No, a *great* time." He tugged my hair hard.

I screamed as my head was yanked back.

Vasant shoved the bottle's neck into my mouth and poured the wine down my throat.

I was at a tavern in the White City, talking to the owner about cooking meals for the refugees, for a price, of course, when Douve, a castle guard, found me.

"My king." He bowed his head low. "King Vasant is at the White Palace."

"What?" I barked. I had received a report that Vasant had crossed the border, but according to him, they were just taking a shortcut to the Dusk Court, where Vasant had something important to do.

So had he lied, or decided to make a short visit while here? More than that, was he stupid? He knew I didn't like him, like most of the other kings and queens. Thirty years ago, Vasant had started the civil war that ravaged the Spring Court, and after fifteen years of fighting, he had killed his older brother, the actual king, and his entire family, and then he took the throne for himself. The other kings, queens, and I only tolerated him when we needed to discuss important matters about Wyth as a whole; otherwise, we preferred him to stay away.

Which meant I hated having the bastard in my palace.

Especially with Amber in there. If Vasant saw Amber....

Desperation grew inside my chest. To be faster, I shifted into my wolf form and dashed toward the White Palace, with my six knights following closely.

I ran into the palace and took a long sniff. Amber's sweet, flowery scent was everywhere in the palace by now, but I could easily identify where it was strongest, meaning she was either there, or had just been. I followed her scent, skidding through the hallways until I burst into the dining room.

When I saw Amber on a chair, her arms and legs tied by vines, and Vasant leaning over her, pouring a bottle of wine down her throat, I lost it. I rammed into him, pushing him away from her. He fell to the floor, skidding several feet away, his crown on the floor. The bottle, almost empty, shattered on the floor, sending millions of shards everywhere.

Startled, Vasant rolled back, snatched his crown, and shot up, his magic at his fingertips. "Cadewyn!" He smiled at me but didn't drop his magic. "I heard you had a human pet, but I didn't know she was so tempting. Glad I stopped by so I could play with her."

I shifted back into my fae form. "Don't you dare touch her again," I said, my voice low, barely controlled. If he said the wrong thing, if he moved the wrong way, I would kill him. Snow above, I would rip his chest open. That act would start a new war, but right then, I didn't care about that. All I cared about was getting this bastard away from Amber.

"Despite the new toy, I came here on business," Vasant said.

I snorted. "You really think I want to talk business with you, Vasant?"

"It's important." He let go of his magic and straightened

his back, becoming serious, more serious than I had seen him in years. "I want to talk about an alliance."

"Do you hear yourself?" I shook my head. "You know I despise you. And to make everything worse, you came into my house and messed with my people." I forced myself to be civil, for my court's sake. If we started a war right now, we would be doomed. "Get the frost out of my palace, Vasant."

"Cadewyn, hear—"

"GET THE FROST OUT!"

My White Knights rushed forward and flanked Vasant.

With a huff, Vasant let my knights escort him out. As he walked by Amber, who was practically passed out on the chair, he spat at her feet. I clenched my hands, trying to contain my rage.

I can't start a war. I can't start a war.

I kept telling myself that on repeat until he walked out of the dining room. The moment he was out of sight, the vines around Amber disappeared and her limp body slid to the floor. With my fast reflexes, I picked her up in my arms before she hit the hard stone floor.

Both of Amber's guards entered the room through the kitchen, their heads low.

"Where the frost were you two?" I asked, my anger barely contained.

"A thousand apologies, my king," Niossal said, staring at his feet. "I left to go check on what was going on and to find you. Meanwhile, Vasant took charge of things. When the handmaid and the guard tried to interfere, he hurt the handmaid and threatened Lady Amber. He said he would kill Lady Amber if we interrupted him again."

The freezing bastard!

I let out a long, exasperated breath. "How's the handmaid?"

"She's fine now, my king," Niossal said. "Scared and a little hurt but fine."

I nodded, reminding myself that the danger was gone. Everyone would be fine now, even Amber. "Good. Tell her to rest. I'll personally check on her tomorrow." My brows slanted down. "Amber might be a temporary guest, but while she's here, she belongs in the Winter Court. Next time someone threatens her or hurts her, you better defend her as one of our own. Keep the threat, even if it's a king, back until I get to you. I'll deal with the consequences later."

"Yes, my king," the guards said in unison.

Just then, Amber moaned in my arms, totally drunk on fae wine. Vasant, that bastard.... I couldn't even begin to think what he would have done to her if I hadn't arrived here, if I had arrived too late.

I shook my head, sending those thoughts away.

Holding Amber in my arms, I marched out of the dining room, through the hallways, and into her bedroom. The guards closed the door behind me, leaving us alone.

I gently sat her up in her bed. Her head fell on my shoulder.

"Amber, can you hear me?"

Her green eyes opened and zeroed in on my face, though I was sure she was seeing two or three of me. Fae wine was too strong for humans. They got drunk instantly, and if ingested in large doses, it could kill.

"Cade," she whispered my name, making my insides twist in knots. "You're here."

I smoothed my hand in her messy hair. "I'm here now. I won't let anyone hurt you again." No one besides me. Because

I had to hurt her. In the end, I would be the one to hurt her the most.

I dropped my hand.

Amber smiled at me. "I missed you." My breath caught. I still couldn't breathe when she snaked her hand up my chest and around my shoulder. "I know you ran away because of the kiss, but I missed you." Her lips turned down. "I must be a terrible kisser to make you run away from me like that. I'm so sorry for making you stay away from your own home."

"You didn't make me stay away," I lied. I had stayed away because of her, but not for the reason she believed.

"It has been—" She pulled her hand back and stared at it, counting on her fingers. "—three, five, nine, a million days!" Her voice pitched high, sounding funny. It brought a smile to my face. Amber pointed at me. "Look! Holy shit, you're smiling. I could have sworn you didn't know how to smile."

"I do know how to smile." And she was the one I wanted to smile at the most. But it wasn't right. Snow above, it wasn't right. I forced my smile away. "The fae wine will make you feel terribly sick soon. You should lie down and rest now."

I leaned forward, reaching for her shoes. While I was taking them off, Amber hugged my back. I stilled.

"I wish you didn't have to go," she whispered. "I wish you didn't hate me so much that you have to go."

Those words. Any of her words. They always ripped at my chest, causing me more pain.

Gently, I leaned back and pulled her arms from around me. "You're tired, Amber. Rest."

She pouted, and for a second all I wanted was to close the distance between us and taste those lips again. "I don't want to rest. I'm not tired."

I held on to her hands and helped her lie down in her

bed. "Yes, you are. You just don't notice it yet. You should go to sleep, so you don't feel too sick later."

She rested her head on the pillow and closed her eyes. "But I don't want to."

I sat beside her, watching as she tucked her hands under her cheek and her breathing gradually slowed.

I reached up and smoothed her hair back, my fingers lingering on her neck. "I'll tell you something, but only because you won't remember tomorrow." I ran my fingertips down her throat and traced her collarbone. "I'm falling for you, Amber. That's why I stayed away. You see, I can't fall for you, because if I do, I won't be able to save my people, and as a king, my people have to come first. Always." I paused, watching her beautiful face, so at peace while she slept. "But you make me hesitate. You make me wish there was another way. But there isn't. There isn't, and this is killing me." I retreated my hand but lay on the bed beside her, my eyes glued to her face. "You have to die, but you're the one killing me."

For now, I stayed beside her, making sure her sleep was peaceful, that she didn't get too sick in the middle of the night.

I would figure out the rest—my heart, my agony, my dilemma—tomorrow.

A NASTY HEADACHE assaulted me when I sat up in bed. The sun was already high, but I couldn't even look at the window because it made my head hurt more.

What the hell happened?

Then it all rushed back to my mind.

Vasant, the vines, the wine. Then Cade in his fierce wolf form sending Vasant off. Cade carrying my super drunk self to my bedroom. Me saying all sorts of embarrassing things, while he insisted I go to sleep. I had been way too drunk with fae wine, but I remembered most of it.

I buried my face in my hands, mortified.

"Good morning!" a chirpy voice said.

Eyes wide, I lifted my head and found someone I knew but hadn't met yet. "Mahaere," I whispered, staring at the goddess. She was more beautiful than the drawings in the books. Actually, she looked just like Mahaera—the same face, the same body shape—the only things that changed were the hair, the clothes, and the personality. Mahaere's hair was bright red, tied in a loose ponytail on the top of her head. She wore a red tunic over red leggings and high-heeled red boots. Supposedly, she was the fun sister, loud and bright.

"So you heard about me," she said, picking up a tray from the table on the other side of the room. She brought the tray to me. "I hope it was all good things."

I stared at her, not sure what to tell her. "Hmm...."

"Don't worry, silly." She put the tray on the mattress beside me and waved me off. "I'm playing with you." She gestured to the tray. "You should eat your breakfast and drink this." She lifted a small glass with a sickly green liquid. "Medicine. It tastes bad but will help with your headache and overall hangover."

I stared at the food. It all looked great, but at the same time, my stomach twisted. "I don't think I can eat right now."

"Just take this, then." Mahaere put the small glass with medicine in my hand. She watched me expectantly, so I forced myself to take it. It tasted horrible. I gagged but was able to keep it down. She patted my leg. "You'll feel better in no time, you'll see."

"Hm." I glanced around, remembering Cade was in my bedroom last night before I went to sleep. After that, I hadn't seen or heard anything. Had he left again? Had my shameful confession sent him away again? "Do you know about...?"

"King Cadewyn?" Mahaere asked, expectantly.

"Yes," I said. Her bluntness made me a little twitchy, but at the same time, it was nice not to have to go around in circles. "Did he leave again?"

"Yes and no. Early morning he left the palace to go to the White City, but he'll be back soon. He asked me to tell you he'll come see you after the cleansing ritual." My cheeks warmed. Mahaere hopped off the bed. "Now, let's get you ready. I'll walk with you to the Moon Temple." She beckoned me to follow her. "Come on."

A little disconcerted because of the headache, Mahaere's intensity, and the fact Cade had left a message for me, I climbed off the bed and followed Mahaere to the closet. She wanted me to put on gowns that should be used in fancy balls or skimpy ones that certainly belonged in the bedroom. In the end, I chose one that was simple but elegant, with a light-blue fabric and white and silver details. Though I let Mahaere talk me into pulling my hair back into an intricate braid.

I couldn't wrap my mind around the fact that a fae goddess was acting like my girlfriend and braiding my hair, but from the little I knew about her, she was always genuine about her enthusiasm. She was so enthusiastic, in fact, that some of it rubbed off on me.

By the time we went to the Moon Temple, I felt much better and less anxious about meeting Cade later. I couldn't freaking wait.

I HADN'T EXPECTED to see Cade as soon as I stepped out of the Moon Temple, but there he was, looking so stoic and powerful and hot as ever, standing in the middle of the stone path. Didn't the man own a shirt? I had seen him wearing one before. I might have to tell him he better wear shirts when around me.

His light-blue eyes were fixed on me as I walked to him.

"How are you feeling?" he asked, his voice rough as always.

"Better." The embarrassment for the previous night came

back with full strength. "I'm sorry if I said and did things last night that—"

"There's nothing to be sorry about," Cade said, interrupting me. His thick brows slammed down. "I'm the one who has to apologize. Amber, I'm so sorry about Vasant and what he did to you. I promise you, nothing like that will ever happen again."

I was glad to hear that, though he didn't owe me anything. "Thank you."

Cade cleared his throat. "I was wondering if you would like to go out for a ride with me. There's a place I would like to show you."

It was hard to curb my excitement. "I would love that."

Cade offered me his arm, and I took it.

MOUNTED ON BLIZZARD, we rode through the White City then turned north at the road. We skirted a small village, went a couple more miles, and finally arrived at a valley covered in snow.

Cade brought Blizzard to a stop and pointed down. "Right there."

I followed his finger and tried to find whatever he was pointing at. Right in the middle of the valley was a small lake with smoke rising from the water's surface. I gasped. "A hot water spring."

Cade nodded. "Something like that. It's the only one in the entire Winter Court."

He kicked Blizzard's sides, and the horse started moving again, sending him down the valley on a hidden path at a much slower pace.

Cade let out a long breath.

I frowned. "What's wrong?"

"A lot of things," he said in a low voice, surprising me. I hadn't expected him to actually answer me. "The curse took two villages already and is quickly advancing on a third. In the past few days, I've been evacuating the residents, bringing them to the White City and making sure they are comfortable."

"So that was why you were away," I mused.

Cade nodded once. "I'm worried, though. The White City is right in the center of the Winter Court. If the curse speeds up again, we might have to evacuate from there too."

"Is there a way to hold the ceremony sooner? Like, I don't know, tomorrow?"

"I actually asked Mahaeru that yesterday," he said. "She told me you're still not ready for it. You need at least a few more cleansing rituals."

I didn't understand about the need for a cleansing ritual and this other bigger ceremony, but I wasn't fae. I would never understand everything they did and felt and needed.

Even so, I could sympathize with all the misfortune falling over the Winter Court.

I rubbed my hand down his back, comforting him. "I'm sorry."

"It's okay. You're doing everything you can. We all are."

A moment later, we arrived at the hot spring area. Even from a distance, we could feel the warmth of the water, making the air foggy and the bank of the lake snowless.

We hopped off Blizzard right where the snow ended and the grainy sand started.

I looked around. I could see a lot of snow covering the

valley, and the mist from the hot lake, but not much more. Despite that, this place felt peaceful. "I like it here."

"You'll like it even more in the water," Cade said, unbuckling the leather strap from across his chest. His heavy fur cloak fell to the ground.

My eyes bugged. "What?"

He fixed his eyes on mine; so meaningful, they took my breath away. "Come into the water with me," he said before stripping off his pants. Cheeks suddenly very hot, I averted my eyes. When I heard splashing in the distance, I dared look at him again. He was deep into the lake, the water at his chest. "Come."

How could I resist when he called me like that?

My body shook as I slowly took off my coat and slipped off my dress. The chilly wind brushed against me, but right then my body was becoming so hot, it didn't bother me.

I bit the inside of my cheek, pausing for a moment. Then I quickly took off my bra and panties and trudged into the water—all the while under the careful, lustful gaze of the waiting fae king.

That look, the shine in his eyes, it emboldened me somehow. I felt sexy and in control as I walked deeper into the hot water, amazed by the nice, warm temperature, but more amazed that *this* was happening.

I halted a few feet away from him.

His eyebrows slanted down. "Why are you so far away?" He reached forward, grabbed my arm, and pulled me to him. No pauses, no waiting, no hesitation. I crashed into him, his rock-hard body against mine, and then his hands were on my back and his mouth closed on mine.

A moan slithered from my throat when I felt his erection against my lower stomach. My core clenched with anticipation. Holy shit, was this really happening? Would he really have sex with me? Would this hot, powerful fae king claim my virginity?

His lips moved fast and urgently against mine, as if he needed to do this quickly before I faded away. I was sure I would have a bruise tomorrow, but I didn't care. As long as he extinguished the increasing fire in my body, I didn't care.

His hands slid down my hips, and I lifted my legs, knotting them around his waist.

"Snow above," Cade muttered against my lips. He pulled away and unwrapped my legs from around him. A pang cut through my chest. Was he rejecting me again? Right now? Suddenly, he turned me around and pressed my back against his chest and my ass against his hard-on. I swallowed hard. "I want to do something first," he whispered in my ear.

He snaked an arm across my chest, his hand closing over my breast. His fingers played with my nipple, and I moaned, sure I would melt away. Then his other hand slid down, down, down. His fingertips trailed across my bellybutton, over the little bush of short hair, and into my center. Whimpering, I bucked against his touch, rubbing my ass on his cock. He groaned in my ear, his breath washing over my neck.

Holy shit!

When I thought this couldn't get any better, he showed me more. Cade slipped a finger inside me, and I gasped.

"Is this good?" he asked, his voice low, husky.

"Yes," I panted as he slipped another finger inside me and started moving them in and out, in and out, in and out.

Moaning, I laid the back of my head on his shoulder and reached behind me, closing my hands around his hard, round ass.

Cade growled in my ear. "What do you want me to do?"

He thrust his hips into my ass, rubbing his erection against me. "Is this what you want?"

"Yes," I whispered. "Give me everything."

I was lost in a sea of pleasure, sure I would explode into pieces at any second.

Then Cade surprised me again. He pressed his thumb against my clit. A jolt rushed through my body, and I cried out. "How about like this?" He moved his thumb, drawing circles around my clit while maintaining the pressure.

I opened my mouth, but only moans came out. I couldn't speak. I had lost my voice, my bearings, my mind. All I had in mind was Cade's fingers and the incredible way they made me feel.

My core tightened, my vagina clenched, the heat increased, and the moans faltered. "That's it. Come for me, Amber," Cade whispered, flicking his thumb over my clit and pumping inside me, deep and hard.

As if his words were a command, my world shattered and I came. My legs gave way, and my body trembled. If Cade didn't have an arm locked around me, I would have slipped under the water.

Without giving me a moment to breathe, Cade spun me around and lowered his mouth to mine, kissing me long and deep. I melted into his arms, sure I had found paradise. Holy shit, what was this? What was this feeling, this pleasure, this heat, this man, this moment? It was just perfect, and I needed more. I needed more of Cade.

Then, Cade broke the kiss and went completely still.

I frowned. "What happened?"

"Shh, I don't want you to be alarmed," he said in a low voice. "But there's someone watching us."

CADE

AMBER TURNED her blue eyes to me. Her face paled. "W-What?"

I smoothed her wet hair back. "I don't think they are friendly."

"They?"

I nodded once. "Yes, there's more than one." And they were trying to be very quiet, but I guess they didn't realize that with my powers I could hear the wind better than anyone, and the wind brought their tense breathing back to me.

What upset me the most was the timing. Did they have to come just now? Just when I had Amber exactly where I wanted? The sound of her moans, her wet center, her ass brushing against my cock—

I was still hard, and now I would have to either run away or fight.

"What will we do?" Amber asked.

"Listen to me," I said. "I want you to act normal. Go to the shore and get dressed. I'll—"

"You want me to get out of the water? Like this?" She gestured to her body. Her hot, naked body.

"Do you prefer waiting for them to come into the water?"

Her eyes grew even bigger. "All right, I'll do it. And then what?"

"We'll hop on Blizzard and gallop away as fast as we can." I slipped my hand into hers and squeezed. "Do you trust me?"

Amber nodded. "I do."

Snow above... I was touched by her trust. I was touched by everything she was and believed and did. How I wished she didn't believe me. How I wished she knew better and ran away from me too.

But I couldn't worry about that now.

There were enemies surrounding us, and I couldn't risk having her in the middle of a battle, even a small one. She was human, after all, and easily hurt. I had to make sure she was safe.

"Ready? Let's do it."

We trudged out of the hot water, the cold air burning our skin. I quickly pulled her coat over her shoulders to hide her body from whoever was watching us. She pulled up her dress, and when she was fully dressed, I shoved on my pants and pulled my cloak over my shoulders.

I forced the wind to whirl faster around the valley, bringing me more sounds. Their breathing and almost silent footsteps were closer.

I reached for Blizzard's reins and helped Amber up into the saddle. The wind whipped again, telling me they were even closer.

"Just go," I told Amber before slapping Blizzard's side and sending him away.

"What? No!" Amber cried, fumbling to hold on to the reins.

Twelve monsters from the Tywyll Forest emerged from the snow, just a few feet from me. They bared their jagged teeth in what looked like a smile, then took off after Amber.

My stomach dropped.

They weren't here for me.

They were here for her.

I shifted into a wolf and ran after them. I caught up with the first in two seconds and ripped him to shreds. The next one was just as fast. But by the time I got the third one, one of the monsters jumped at Blizzard and grabbed Amber. I killed the third one quickly and ran toward Amber as she and the monster fell to the ground, rolling on the snow.

But before I could reach her, two monsters turned to me. I summoned my magic. Ice stakes rose from the snow and pierced their bodies right in the center. In that time, I had already jumped on the back of another monster and bitten off his head.

The remaining five monsters stood before their leader and Amber, as if they could stop me. I almost pitied them when I summoned the wind to create small tornadoes around them, taking all their air away.

The leader held on to Amber, one of his arms around her torso, and the other on her throat, his claws pressing against her skin. She jerked against his grip, trying to kick him and strike him with her elbow, but he only held her tighter.

I shifted back into my fae form. "Let. Her. Go."

"Let her go?" the monster said, leering at me. His yellow, reptile eyes blinked too fast, and his forked tongue ran over his thin lips. "I want to kill her." He pressed his claws deeper into Amber's throat. She whimpered as blood trickled down her skin.

I created a hurricane behind me. "Let. Her. Go."

"Don't you see, King Cadewyn? I'm doing you a favor." His tongue peeked out again. "I heard you'll need to kill her in the near future to save your people, and I'm killing her now."

Amber's eyes became two huge balls. "W-What?"

Snow above....

"Oh, wait," the monster said, tsking. "You need her alive until then, don't you? Too bad. To prevent you from breaking the curse, I need to kill her now."

He pressed his claws to her throat harder.

And I threw my hand out, willing a spear of ice to appear and zip toward him.

It sank right into his chest, just an inch from Amber's shoulder.

Still holding on to Amber, the monster croaked and crumpled to the ground. Amber was able to disentangle herself from him, but she stumbled back and fell on the snow.

She stared from the dead monster to me, her big eyes full of fear.

"Amber," I whispered, not sure what to say, what to tell her. This wasn't how I had imagined it all going. "Please, don't look at me like that."

She scooted back on the snow. "Stay away from me." She got up and retreated a few more steps. "Is it true? What he said, is it true?"

I let out a long sigh. "Yes," I confessed, my heart heavy. "Mahaera told me that to stop the curse, I had to sacrifice the life of a pure-hearted, selfless human. She said that when I went to Earth, I would know who would be fit to fulfill the sacrifice. The moment I saw you, I knew. Back then, I didn't think twice. I just brought you here and—"

"You tricked me," she spat. "You brought me here and you had me believe that I was helping you, that all I had to do was go through some cleansing rituals so I could help you save your people, and then I would go back home. You never mentioned I had to die!"

I ran a hand over my wet hair. "I'm sorry." It was all I could say. "I'm so sorry."

Amber shook her head. "I don't care. I'm going back home." She turned her back to me and started marching away—barefoot in the snow.

Snow above, this was all messed up.

I wanted to respect her and give her some time before I tried explaining my reasoning to her, before I tried telling her that I couldn't bear the thought of killing her, of losing her, but if I left her alone in the snow like that, she would either die of hypothermia before she reached the next village, or she could be attacked again. From what I understood from the monsters, the Tabred clan had figured out her role in my court, and they would stop at nothing to kill her before she was ready for the ceremony—before I could save my land.

I didn't make her faint this time, but I did wrap my arm around her waist and bring her up on Blizzard with me. She yelled, she kicked, she punched, but I was much stronger than her. With me holding her firmly, she wouldn't go anywhere.

Halfway back to the White Palace, Amber stopped fighting. Instead, she curled into herself and started crying in silence.

My heart broke for her.

I QUICKLY REALIZED I couldn't fight or outrun Cade. So I gave up. I didn't try running from him when we dismounted at the White Palace's gardens, or when he brought me inside and locked me in my bedroom.

Before I had felt like an esteemed guest. Now, I was a prisoner.

I wondered...did everyone know I was to be sacrificed for their court? Did they know and pretended they didn't when they looked me in the eye, talked to me, laughed with me, brought me food, cooked with me?

I felt betrayed, humiliated.

I glanced around my bedroom. How could I escape? The door was locked, and even if I could open it, there were at least two guards outside. The window was too high, and I would break my entire body, or die, if I tried to jump.

Stubborn, I opened the windows and looked out. The exterior of the palace resembled sleek ice. There were no places for me to use as footholds. There was no way to climb down.

Not willing to give up just yet, I started knocking and pushing on the walls around the room, trying to find some secret opening. But nothing budged.

I was truly locked in here.

I sat down on my bed, accepting the truth. Even if I found a way of escaping the palace, I had no way of returning to Earth. I needed one of those medallions Cade had to open a portal and go back to the human world.

A deep pain started inside my chest.

Why, oh why did it have to be this way? Cade and I had just shared an amazing moment. I had never done anything like that in my entire life, never felt like that. I thought we had really connected. For a brief moment, I had let myself believe I was in paradise, and when this ceremony thing ended, Cade would ask me to stay in Wyth with him.

Then I learned the truth, and my heart shattered into a million pieces.

A knock came from the door, startling me. I ignored it. If it was the handmaids with dinner, I had lost my appetite. If it was Cade, I really didn't want to see him right then.

The knock came again. "Amber, it's Chiara."

I thought about ignoring her, but she had been very kind to me so far, even if she probably knew I had to die to save her court. My pure and selfless heart couldn't just shut her down.

"I want to be alone right now," I said.

"I know. I just wanted to let you know that I didn't know. Nobody knew. They still don't. Cade only told me because he was raging in his bedroom and I went to confront him." She paused. "I'm so sorry, Amber. I really didn't know. I wish.... I wish I could find another way."

"Chiara, go away." A tear rolled down my face. "Please."

No knock followed. No more words. I assumed Chiara really left. Another tear escaped my eyes. Then another.

I wiped my face, upset with myself for crying. I should be raging, breaking things, threatening them to make them let me go.

What good would that do? I had already concluded that I couldn't escape, unless I stole a medallion, and I couldn't see that happening.

Defeated, I crawled to the pillows at the head of the bed, hugged them, and tried to sleep, because that was the only way to forget.

THE NEXT MORNING, I didn't get up from bed, but I sat up when a different handmaid came in, holding a tray with breakfast.

"Where's Tiana?" I asked.

"She's sick, my lady." The female fae lowered her head. "My name is Delia. I'll be her replacement until she's better." She put the tray on the table across the room. "Shall I choose a dress for you, or would you like to do that yourself?"

I lay back in the bed. "There's no need for a dress. I'm not getting out of bed today." Or tomorrow, or the next day, or the day after that.

"But I was told to help you get ready and escort you to the Moon Temple."

I snorted. "I'm not going to the Moon Temple." I was done with this ridiculous cleansing ritual. I was done with the Winter Court and the fae realm. "What you could help me with is a way to escape," I joked.

The handmaid stilled. "Are you serious about that, my lady?"

I sat up and stared at her. "What if I am?"

"Well...." The young fae approached my bed. "The truth is, I'm here as a spy."

I gasped. She looked like a teenager, but I knew fae aged differently than humans. She was probably older than me. Still, the fact that she was a spy amidst so many powerful fae bothered me for some reason. "A spy," I said calmly, even though I was suddenly wary of her. If she was sent here among so many wolves, it was because she could take care of herself.

"Yes, my lady. I work for Grimmel, the leader of the Tabred clan."

I scooted back from her as fear snaked down my spine. "Your leader tried to have me killed yesterday."

I opened my mouth to call the guards, but then she said, "I know, my lady, and I apologize for that. My lord thought that was the only way, but I'm here to offer you another solution."

I frowned. "What solution?"

"All my lord wants is to stop the ceremony," she said. "If he had you killed before the ceremony, the curse wouldn't be broken, and his plan would succeed. But there's another way. If I help you escape, I can take you somewhere safe, where you can take a portal and go back to the human world."

"But...." Despite the craziness of what she was saying, I thought about it for a moment. "Cade would come get me again."

"You can either hide in the human world or with us until the time for the ceremony is past and the curse has taken the Winter Court. We'll keep you safe."

I was angry with Cade. Actually, anger was just one of the many feelings swirling inside me right then. I was sad, lost, desperate, disappointed, frustrated.... I had never felt so much in so little time. Despite it all, I didn't wish the Winter Court to be wiped out completely.

But what other choice did I have? Stay here and wait to die? Or run away and let the Winter Court be destroyed?

It was an impossible choice for me. And for once, I wanted to be selfish. Until a few days ago, I didn't even know this world existed. Now I had to die in order to save it? That wasn't fair.

I bit the inside of my cheek, completely lost. "Let me think about it."

Delia pressed her lips tight. "All right. Since we still have time, we'll talk about it tomorrow." She gestured to the closet. "Now, what will you wear today?"

I turned my back to her and lay back in bed, hugging my pillow. "Nothing. Like I told you before, I won't go to that stupid cleansing ritual, and I definitely won't get out of bed all day."

"As you wish," Delia said.

Two seconds later, I heard the door opening and closing. Delia had exited, leaving me alone with my agony.

And the three thousand thoughts in my mind. What should I do now?

CADE

EVERY CELL in my body screamed for me to go to Amber's bedroom and check if she was okay, but I stopped myself, because I knew I would only make everything worse. She wasn't ready to talk yet. Honestly, I wasn't sure she would ever be.

Her new handmaid told me she had refused to go to the Moon Temple this morning, as I expected. Then, Mahaera showed up in my study as I paced across the floor, sure soon I would leave markings on the hard, white stone. She assured me that missing one cleansing ritual in the middle of them all wouldn't be a problem.

"Are you sure there's no other way to stop this curse?" I asked Mahaera again. I probably had asked her that a thousand times now.

"I'm sure," she said, her tone curt.

There were so many other problems, though. I was beside myself that Grimmel had sent assassins to kill Amber, which meant he would try it again. And now Amber knew about her purpose here, and she hated me. I didn't know which problem was the worst.

During the day, I tried occupying my mind with useful things, like helping and organizing the latest evacuations, setting up new spaces for the new refugees, and finding activities for them to do. Soon, we would run out of space in the White City.

Soon, we would have to evacuate the White City.

By the end of the day, my body and mind were exhausted. My body from working nonstop, and my mind from trying to find a magical solution—how could I save my court *and* Amber at the same time?

My heart was heavy when I went back to the palace late that night. I hadn't even realized my feet had betrayed me until I stopped right in front of the doors to Amber's bedroom.

The guards bowed to me.

"Has she left her bedroom today?"

"No, my king," Niossal said. "And all trays of food came back untouched."

Snow above, what was she doing? Protesting about her fate? Didn't she know by now that I also hated it? That I didn't want to go through with the sacrifice? That my heart was being ripped in two?

No, she probably didn't know.

So I decided to tell her about it.

I unlocked the door and went in. Since it was so late, I had expected to find the room dark and Amber sleeping. Instead, the lamps on the nightstands were on, giving the room a cool, dim white shine, and Amber was seated in her bed, her back to me.

I closed the door behind me and took two steps toward her bed.

"I already told you, I'm not hungry," she said, her voice devoid of any emotion. "You can take the tray back, Delia. And take that one too." She pointed to the table across the room, where a tray full of food sat untouched.

"I'm not Delia," I said, my voice calm. I wanted to remain calm for as long as I could. I doubted it would last two minutes.

Amber shot up from the bed and retreated to the window. "What are you doing here?" She clutched the long bathrobe, and just then I realized her hair was damp. She had just taken a shower.

Snow above, was she naked underneath that robe? I shook my head, pushing those thoughts away. This wasn't the time to think about that. "I heard you haven't eaten all day. I wanted to make sure you're all right."

She crossed her arms. "Do you think I'm all right?"

I let out a long sigh. "I know you're not." I advanced two more steps, and Amber retreated one more, her thighs bumping on the low windowsill. "Amber, I know you don't want to talk to me right now, or even look at me, but I have something to say, and I need you to listen to me. You don't need to say anything, just hear me out, okay?"

"As if saying no will stop you," she muttered.

Right. It wouldn't. "When I first saw the curse and Mahaera came to me, saying only the sacrifice of a pure-hearted and selfless human would stop it, I didn't think twice. I went to Earth right away and looked for the one who I would have to kill." She winced. "I found you, and since the first time I laid my eyes on you, I felt divided about my mission. I pushed through, because I was raised to put my court above everything else, and brought you here. Things would have been much easier if we could have performed the ceremony right away. I admit that if that was the case, then I would have hesitated, but I would have done it. I would have killed you."

"Just for the record, whatever you're trying to accomplish here, you're way off the mark," Amber protested.

I went on. "Because we have to wait for the ceremony, I got to spend time with you. I got to know you. You really are selfless and pure-hearted, like no one else on Earth or Wyth. And on top of all that, you're so beautiful, I become breathless every time I look at you." From here, I heard her heartbeat speeding up. "I don't want to kill you, Amber, not before, not now, but I'm at my wit's end. I want to save you *and* my court, but it seems I have to choose one. This is too hard," I admitted, surprised with my own words. I hadn't expected to say all that to her. But it was the truth. She deserved the truth. "Tell me... tell me you want to live. I'll open a portal for you right now and let you go."

Amber buried her face in her hands. I heard soft sniffs coming from her. My body itched to go to her and embrace her and tell her everything would be okay, even if that was a lie. The biggest lie of my life.

Finally, she hugged herself and faced me. "I can't just leave," she said. "Do you think I want the fact that I doomed your kingdom on my conscience? How will I go on everyday knowing your land is gone because of me?" A soft sob rose from her throat. "But I don't want to die either." She shrugged. "I don't know what to do."

I lost the battle against my self-control. I went to her and wrapped my arms around her, pulling her to me, tight and safe. She buried her face in my chest, and I stroked her long, damp hair down her back.

"I want to tell you everything will be okay, but I'd be lying, and I don't want to lie to you anymore." I kissed the top of her head. "What I can honestly tell you is that I will do all I can to keep you safe for as long as I can."

She pulled back just one inch, wiped the tears from her face, and looked up at me. "Will you do something for me?"

"Anything," I said, being honest. Aside from giving up my court, which I knew she would never ask me to do, I would do anything for her.

Her cheeks turned bright red. "Sleep with me." I stared at her, shocked by her blunt request. "I'm...." She paused, her cheeks redder by the second. "I'm a virgin, and I wouldn't like to die a virgin."

Sympathy and pure lust battled in my chest. I cupped her face. "I need to believe you won't die. Not tomorrow, not next week, not in a hundred years." I sucked in a sharp breath. "As for your request...are you sure?"

She pulled away, making my arms drop to my sides. "It's okay if you don't want it. Pretend you didn't hear me."

"You're kidding me, right?" I snaked an arm around her waist and pulled her to me. "I've been dying to sleep with you since I first laid eyes on you. I just don't want you to regret it tomorrow."

She chuckled, as if I had said something absurd. "Cade, I doubt I would regret anything about you."

Those words...they got a grip around my heart and squeezed hard. Then they went south, directly to my cock. My pants were suddenly too snug.

"You've been warned," I said, before lowering my head and pressing my lips to hers.

Every thought in my head was about taking this slow, enjoying it, savoring Amber and this moment, but every nerve in my body, every drop of blood rushing to my hard-on told me I couldn't take it slow, not when it came down to her.

Amber parted her lips, and I claimed her mouth, teasing her tongue with mine. I found the belt of her robe, unknotted it, opened it a little, and snaked my hands around her waist, drawing her back to me. I ran my hands up and down her back, feeling her silky skin, her thin waist. At the hot spring, I had seen her hot body, I had touched her, but this was different. This time, I would leave a mark on every inch of her.

Amber rolled her shoulders and let her robe fall to the floor. Groaning against her lips, I slid my hands down and around her ass, pulling her up. She knotted her legs around me. I wanted to press her against the wall and take her just like this, but since this was her first time, I had to make sure I was gentle, or as gentle as I could possibly be when my entire body thrummed with so much desperate lust.

I deposited her on the bed and brought her right to the edge. Then I knelt in front of her.

Amber's eyes went wide as she stared me. "What are you—oh!"

I shut her up when I pushed her legs apart and buried my face in her center. "Oh!" Amber bucked her ass, but I held down her legs, keeping her where I wanted her. I drove my tongue around her clit while I slid a finger inside. "Holy shit," she muttered, her voice hoarse. Her surprise, her innocence, her words, they all went directly to my cock, making me harder and harder. I ached to do something about it—to wrap her hands around me, to slide inside her—but I hung on. Now it was her turn to be pleasured.

I slipped another finger inside her and pumped fast and hard while flicking my tongue around her clit.

Her back arched, and her hands knotted into my hair. "Cade, please...."

I lifted my eyes to her. Without stopping my fingers, I pulled back a little and asked, "Please what?"

She groaned, tugging at my hair. "Just...don't stop."

A small smile tugged at my lips before I sank into her again. I swirled my tongue around her clit, eating her in concert with my hand. Her walls clenched around my fingers, her entire body tightening, her breathing pausing.

Her body shook as she came.

Satisfied with what I had done to her, I pulled my fingers from her and brought them to my mouth, tasting her. Sweet, warm, tangy. My hunger for her only increased.

I watched her while I took off my clothes—thrown over the bed, her hair a long fan around her head, drunken with her ecstasy. She was beautiful. So hot, I could stare all day long, all year long, and I would never get tired of her.

My cock jerked, angry at me for just standing there. Slowly, I crawled over her. She blinked her pretty green eyes and stared at me, her gaze skimming over my body. Her dazed eyes suddenly sobered when she saw my erection, all thick and pointing at her.

Hands splayed on the sides of her head, I held myself over her, my ankles touching her feet but nothing else. I could hear her shallow breathing and her heart racing a million miles per hour.

"Are you nervous?"

She moved her eyes to mine and shook her head for two seconds, then nodded. "I am, but I want this." Her hands rested on my chest, her fingertips tracing over the outlines of the muscles on my abdomen. "I want you." She slid her hands lower, and I groaned.

But before she could close her hand around my cock, I eased my body against hers, lowering my head to her chest. I ran my tongue over the curve of her breasts, then cupped one with my hand while closing my mouth over the other. Amber whimpered and arched her back, her hands finding my hair again. I sucked at her hard nipple, suddenly feeling like I could make her come with just that.

But the next time she came would be with me inside her.

I dragged my lips over her collarbone and up her neck. Amber's hands migrated to my shoulders. I lifted my head to look at her and poised my shaft at her entrance. She stilled, sucking in a sharp breath.

"Try to relax," I said. Slowly, I inched inside her. Her nails sank into my shoulders, and a mix of pain and pleasure shot through me. When I filled her to the hilt, I stopped, giving her time to adjust to me. But I had to adjust to her too. I groaned. Snow above, she was so wet, so tight, so perfect.

I suppressed a gasp as a tug started in my chest, like a rope tied around my heart, pulling me to her. It was an almost tangible feeling that I had only heard about but until now hadn't felt.

The mating bond.

It had snapped into place.

Amber was my mate.

Eyes wide, I stared at her.

This pure-hearted, selfless, beautiful human was my mate.

I let out a growl as a protective feeling assaulted me—I had wanted to protect her before, but not like this. Snow above, this time, it was mixed with such an intense possessiveness, it left me baffled.

I brought my mouth to hers, and she parted her lips for me. I gently kissed her as I worshipped her.

She was *mine*. All mine.

Amber broke the kiss, throwing her head back as she wiggled under me.

"Are you okay?" I asked, worried about her. She stilled again. Eyes closed, mouth open, she nodded. "Does it hurt?" She shook her head. I took that as a hint to start moving. I was gentle at first, sliding in and out of her.

I was having sex with my mate.

No, I was making love with my mate. Just that knowledge was enough to draw the beast out of me. I wanted more. I wanted all of her. I *needed* her.

She drew in little breaths each time I filled her, but after a moment, she ran her nails over my back. "Faster," she whispered.

Snow above. "My pleasure."

I sped up, the friction of her wet, tight pussy around my cock almost too much. I hadn't been with a woman in so long, and now I was with my frosting mate! I knew I wouldn't last long. But I wanted to. With Amber, with my fated mate, I wanted to last all night long.

I kissed her again, but this time I wasn't gentle at all. I ravaged her mouth, savoring her sweet taste, inhaling her flowery scent.

"Oh," she whimpered against my mouth. Her hands snaked down my body and grasped my ass, tugging me to her harder. "More," she whispered.

Snow above. I complied—how could I not? I pounded

into her, as fast and deep and hard as I could, the sensation, the emotions, the act, all too much, too fast, too powerful.

A moment later, Amber's pussy clenched around my cock, and her body trembled as she came. I groaned, trying to resist it, to last longer, but it was just too frosting much. I thrust into her once, twice, three times more, and then exploded into her. I buried my head in her shoulder as I rode out the ecstasy.

Amber's arms wound around my shoulders in a tight embrace.

I turned my head to her.

My mate.

Amber was my mate.

"Are you okay?" I asked.

"I think I'm in heaven," she said with a smile.

I chuckled. "There's no heaven in the fae world."

"Then where would I say I am? Because I'm pretty sure you're a god and I'm in a place just like paradise."

I lifted my head and looked at her. Snow above, the feelings inside my chest expanded, and I was sure my heart would burst at any second.

"How about right here with me?" I asked, my voice thick with emotion.

She snuggled against me. "I like that."

I lay beside her and pulled her to me, her delicate, soft body molded around mine. I smoothed her hair down her back and pressed my lips to her forehead. "You must be tired. Go to sleep."

She rested her head on my shoulders and rubbed her nose across my throat, sending a shiver of pleasure down my spine. If she continued like that, I wouldn't be responsible for my actions.

But I had to think about her. It had been her first time, a fact that actually made me so freezing proud. She was probably sore after making love with me.

So I just held her—*my mate*—as her breathing slowed.

And I stared at her, sure I couldn't let her die, no matter what.

20

AMBER

AFTER LAST NIGHT, I didn't expect to wake up alone. I wanted to be upset and disappointed with Cade for leaving me, but the images from last night flooded my mind, and my body grew hot.

Something happened last night, I could feel it. It wasn't just because it had been my first time; no, there had been something more between Cade and me, something I couldn't explain. I knew I liked him before having slept with him. Now, my feelings were tenfold. Just thinking about him made me miss him, made me want him, made me hot for him. It was like there was a connection between us, a pull that drew me to him. I knew it was probably all in my mind, but I couldn't help but wonder.

I hugged the pillow and inhaled deeply, savoring Cade's delicious scent. If I went back home, could I take this pillow with me, so I would always smell Cade?

A sudden sadness fell over me.

I climbed down from the bed, picked up the bathrobe from the floor, put it on, and went to the window. I opened the glass and welcomed the chilly breeze that brushed against me.

This cold wind was part of this kingdom, as were the snowcapped mountains in the distance, the bustling city below, the lively marketplace, the beautiful places I had seen when riding with Cade here and there, and the magic. If I left, if I ran away, all this would be gone.

Cade would be left with a bunch of miserable people without a court.

I couldn't just leave and do nothing. If I could help them to keep this beautiful court from disappearing, then I had to do something.

Though I had never thought of myself as a pure-hearted and selfless person, I had always considered myself to be good. Someone who tried to do good deeds.

I would do a good deed now too.

For this beautiful land, for the amazing king who had stolen my heart and soul, I would die.

Anxious about my decision, I didn't wait for Tania or Delia to come in with breakfast and escort me to the Moon Temple. I ate one of the small honey cakes that had been left on last night's dinner tray, cleaned up, got dressed in a simple light gray dress and my usual white fur coat, and went to the door. Holding my breath, I turned the handle.

And the door opened.

I smiled.

Yesterday, the door had been locked all day, but after last night, I had a feeling Cade would leave the door unlocked this morning.

My guards seemed surprised to see me after over thirty hours of me being locked inside my bedroom.

"Good morning, my lady," Niossal said. "Is there anything I can do for you?"

"Do you know where Cade is?" I asked, a little embarrassed at the question. Had they seen him leaving in the middle of the night? Had they heard us?

"King Cadewyn left your bedroom about one hour ago," Niossal told me. "He said he had a meeting with Mahaera to attend but would soon come back to see you."

I felt a little better now that I knew Cade had left not long ago and that he would be back soon. Perhaps I could use my free time well too. "Let's just go to the Moon Temple," I told him. "I'm ready for this morning's ritual."

The guards bowed their heads and fell into step with me once I started down the hallways.

I was halfway along the stone path that led to the Moon Temple when Delia called out to me. "Lady Amber, wait!" I halted and waited for her. Upon reaching me, she bowed her head for a second. "My lady, I was worried when I went into your bedroom and didn't find you. Would you like me to bring you some breakfast?"

"I already ate," I told her with a smile. Though, I ate too little. I would soon be hungry, but I wanted to wait until Cade came to see me again so we could have a meal together. "I'm fine for now, thanks."

Delia glanced at the guards, who were several feet behind us, then leaned forward and asked in a whisper, "Have you thought about my proposition? Do you want my help to run away from the Winter Court?"

"Yes, I've made my decision. I'm going to stay and die for the Winter Court."

"What?" Delia asked, shocked.

I smiled at her, ready to explain to her about my reasoning, but then she attacked me.

It happened too fast. One moment, she was a fae with white hair, the next her skin peeled away, showing off a slick, gray body. She advanced on me. My guards saw it happening and came to my aid, but she threw her hands toward them, sending a dark powder through the air around them. The guards slowed down and soon tripped on their own feet before falling on the hard, stone path.

With a gasp, I stared at the monster now in front of me. "What the hell are you doing?"

"If you aren't coming of your own accord, I'll take you by force." She blew the same black powder in my face.

It was like a cloud of darkness had fallen over me, making me incredibly sleepy. I tried fighting it, but I couldn't keep my eyes open, let alone move.

In no time, I plunged into the dark.

21

CADE

THIS MORNING, I hadn't wanted to leave Amber alone, but there was something I needed to do: talk to Mahaera, Mahaere, Mahaeru, or all three of them. I went to my study and called on her.

I paced in front of the long white desk, my hands shaking, my breathing accelerated, my heart pounding.

Amber was my mate. She was my beloved fated mate. And she was supposed to die for me and my people. For my court. Was that some sick joke from fate?

Finally, after an hour of pacing and silently cursing the goddesses, Mahaeru showed up in front of me. Of course, the one who wouldn't be moved by my despair was the one who came to talk to me.

"You knew, didn't you?" I asked without wasting time. "You knew from the start that Amber is my fated mate."

Mahaeru knotted her hands behind her back. "I did, but that doesn't change the fact that she's the only one who can save your land."

"I refuse to believe that," I barked, clenching my fists. "Do the same magic Mahaera did on me the last time I went to Earth. I'll go find someone else."

"There is no one else," Mahaeru said, her voice cold. "And even if there was, do you think a selfless person like Amber will let you kill another innocent person in her place?"

My shoulders deflated. "There has to be another frosting way, Mahaeru."

"I've told you a million times: there's no other way."

"There has to be! You know what the mating bond is, what it does to us. Every nerve in my body is telling me to protect Amber, to love her, to keep her safe no matter what. She's a part of me now, someone I can't live without. And yet my duty as king is telling me the same about my people, about my land." I closed my fist and rested it above my heart. "You know that this will kill me. I can't choose. I won't choose."

"You won't have to choose," she said simply.

My brows furrowed. "What does that mean?"

"You'll understand." Then she was gone.

Just like that. She disappeared without even talking to me properly. The despair in my veins spiked. I grabbed a crystal vase from my desk and threw it against the wall.

A sound like an explosion echoed through my study as crystal shards rained down on the floor.

The door burst open, and Kei ran inside. Before he could speak, I waved my hand at him. "It was nothing. Just that crystal vase—"

"That's not it, Cade," he said, his eyes round, shining with urgency.

I stilled. "What is it?"

Kei gestured for someone to enter. Amber's guards marched into my study and knelt before me.

"Forgive us, my king," Niossal said. His brow was bleeding.

"What in the frost are you talking about?"

"That handmaid, Delia. She was a monster from the Tywyll Forest in disguise." He paused as he looked up at me, his face full of agony. "She took Amber."

My world spun. My legs felt weak. My heart squeezed.

No, I hadn't heard him right. It couldn't be.

Kei held my arms and helped me sit down on one of the armchairs in front of my desk, while the guards explained that the handmaid used some kind of black powder to make them sleep. They woke up a while later with a note folded beside them.

Niossal offered the note to me.

Kei took it and handed it to me.

Still out of it, I unfolded the note and read it.

If you want her, come and get her.

Alone.

"It's a trap," Kei said, reading the note over my shoulder. "It's clearly a trap."

I shot to my feet. "I don't care."

"I know she's the only one who can save us, Cade, but think about it." Kei gripped my shoulders. "Grimmel will have you right where he wants you. There will be nothing stopping him. He'll kill Amber, he'll kill you, and the curse will take the entire Winter Court."

I slapped his arms away. "Amber is my mate, Kei." His eyes rounded. Even the guards were shocked to hear that. "I won't let my mate be taken by that vermin. I'm going after her, and I'm going to bring her back." I inhaled deeply. "Then

I'll find a way to stop this frosting curse without killing my mate."

"I didn't know...." Kei stared at me, his eyes big with sympathy. "I'll help you in any way I can."

"Start by bringing me my battle armor."

WHEN I WOKE UP, my heart pounded hard against my rib cage and panic bloomed under my skin. I found myself tied to a pillar in the middle of a large, strange room. The ground, walls, and tall ceiling were smooth in some parts, but most of it seemed like rough stone, as if it had been carved inside a mountain.

Coarse pillars like the one I was tied to lined the room, and right in the middle was some sort of dais with a throne-like chair made of dried and twisted tree branches.

"She's awake!" someone yelled beside me, startling me.

Delia stepped into my line of sight. Her fae form was gone, replaced by a repulsive monster—slick, greenish-gray skin, a long face, even longer limbs, claws for fingers, no hair, yellow eyes that blinked too fast, and razor-sharp teeth. She reminded me of the monsters who had attacked me at the hot spring lake.

Oh, shit. She had brought me to the Tywyll Forest and handed me over to Grimmel, the leader of the Tabred group, on a silver platter.

The panic I had been trying so hard to control escaped and flooded my veins. My arms shook, and my breathing grew shallow in pure fear. This couldn't be happening. I couldn't be here.

My heart sank. Right when I had finally come to terms with what I had to do, I was stolen away.

It seemed on the way here, I had lost my coat, and my dress had several smudged spots, as if I had been dragged through mud. Fighting my fear, I jerked against the rugged rope, rubbing my shoulders, chest, and wrists against it, sending pain shooting through my entire body.

"So, you're the human who can break my curse," someone said.

A tall, man-like monster walked toward me. My stomach knotted at the sight of him. Underneath his crude leather pants and vest, his skin was a dark gray; black veins ran all over his body, his snake-like eyes were bright red, and his ears were long and pointed. He sneered at me, showing off his jagged teeth. He could chomp off my arm in one bite with those. He halted just a couple of feet from me, his foul odor reaching my nostrils and making me gag. He was Grimmel, the leader of the Tabred, I was sure of it.

"I thought my curse couldn't be broken, but if those three witches say your death will do the trick, I believe them. So far, they haven't been wrong once." He tilted his head, his red gaze skimming over my face, my body. "You're pretty for a human. It'll be a shame to kill you."

I inhaled a shuddering breath. I didn't want to die, not just yet. I had accepted the fact that I would be sacrificed to save Cade's court, but if I died now, then his land would be lost.

Desperate, I glanced around my feet, hoping they had left

a knife or a sharp stone close by, so I could use it to cut my ropes. Like at the White Palace, I didn't really think I would get very far, but I needed to try something. Anything. I couldn't just stay tied to this damn pillar and wait for my demise.

I put on a fake bravado and lifted my chin, defying him. "Are you trying to intimidate me?"

Grimmel leaned closer and took a long sniff. "I call smell your fear, human." He sneered at me again. "You're terrified. What are you more terrified of? Dying or seeing King Cadewyn being killed?"

My eyes widened. "W-What?"

"I heard you have the king all hot and bothered," Grimmel said. "So, when Delia took you, she left a note for the king. I invited him to come rescue you alone."

"That's a trap," I said in a low voice.

He let out a hollow laugh. "One Cadewyn surely knows about, but will enter the mountain willingly anyway."

"No!"

Grimmel drew a dagger from its scabbard at his waist and twirled it in his hand. "From what I heard, he's already on his way here."

No, no. In the back of my mind, I prayed to Mahaera, Mahaere, Mahaeru, and any other god or goddess who would listen to me. *Please, don't let Cade come here.*

"In the end, your appearance will have worked even better than I first planned. My first goal was to put an end to the Winter Court. A king can't rule without a kingdom. Cadewyn would be lost and alone. He would become a nobody, and I would have enjoyed seeing his suffering. But now that he's coming for you, I'll enjoy killing him by my own hands a lot more."

I closed my eyes for a moment, wishing, begging, praying more fervently.

With another laugh, Grimmel walked away, Delia at his heels. He sat on his throne, and Delia crouched beside him. They talked in low tones, so all I could hear was the buzz of their voices. A third monster appeared from a dark corner of the wide cavern-like room, just as ugly and nasty as the other two, and joined their conversation.

An urgent feeling grew in my chest. I had to get out of here. Somehow, I had to find a way of escaping, and it had to be before Cade arrived and was killed right in front of me. Even if I made it only to the mouth of the mountain we were inside and found Cade just outside, it would be better than staying here as bait.

I jerked against the ropes again but didn't do more than just gather more bruises around my shoulders, chest, and wrists.

Trying again, I closed my eyes and called on them. *Mahaera, do you hear me? I know you don't want the Winter Court to fall; otherwise you wouldn't have told Cade about me. Mahaere? Mahaeru? Please, help me. Even if it's only by loosening these ropes. Please, help me!*

Maybe the goddesses didn't hear me because I wasn't fae. Or maybe they did hear me but chose to ignore me.

A sob of pure fear rushed through my throat, and enraged tears burned behind my eyes. It couldn't end like this. It couldn't be like this.

Defeated, my body sagged against the ropes.

A moment later, Grimmel rose from his throne, with Delia and the other monster by his side. More monsters entered the cavern through the main archway. They halted in front of the dais and stepped to the side.

Revealing Cade.

My breath caught, and new tears filled my eyes.

He looked every bit like a powerful king in his white leather armor with silver details and a long sword with a crystal hilt across his back. His hair was tied back in a pony-tail, and his blue eyes shot daggers at Grimmel.

"Grimmel," he said, his voice loud and harsh. "I believe you have something of mine."

"Yours," Grimmel said with a nasty smile. "Yours?" Then his smile was gone, and he narrowed his red eyes as if he had realized something. "This little, puny human is your mate?"

My stomach tightened, and my mouth fell open. I was his *what*?

"Yes, Amber is my fated mate," Cade said, his tone firm. Since entering the room, he hadn't looked at me once, and that was killing me. *Come on, Cade. I need you to look at me, to let me know if what you're saying is really true.* "You'll let her go. This is between you and me."

Grimmel clapped his hands and chuckled. "Let her go so she can be sacrificed and save your court, even if you die at my hands? I would rather kill her and see you in despair for the rest of your long life for losing your mate and your land."

Cade drew his sword from his back. "This is my last warn-ing, Grimmel. Let her go, or I'll kill you."

Boisterous laughter echoed through the cavern. "You and what army? My scouts told me you came alone. You can't kill all of us before I kill you."

Cade whirled his sword in his hand. "Let me show you then."

He lunged at Grimmel.

Grimmel roared, baring his teeth and claws.

Delia and the other monster held up spears.

The monster army ran at Cade.

I screamed, fighting against the ropes around me.

Chaos ensued, and for a moment, all I saw was a mass of bodies battling in front of the dais, while Grimmel watched, waiting his turn.

Then a strong wind blew inside the cave, sending half the monsters flying to the other side. Long ice spikes rose from the stone ground, cutting through a handful more of the enemy. Just as more monsters carrying spears ran into the room, ice covered my ropes.

I gasped, realizing what Cade was doing. With renewed strength, I pushed against the ropes. It took a few tries, but they finally broke. A sense of freedom hit me, but I underestimated how hurt and weak I was and almost fell when I tried walking forward.

"Amber, run!" Cade yelled from amidst the fray.

I stared at him, wielding his sword and cutting through the monsters. He continued using his magic to blow them away or cut through them with ice. He truly looked like the fiercest warrior in a romance book, and once more I wondered if I hadn't stumbled into a fairy tale, one of those tragic ones where the lovers died at the end.

No, I wouldn't think about that now.

I racked my mind, trying to come up with a plan. Should I run like Cade wanted me to and leave him alone to deal with these monsters? Would he be able to kill them all and kill Grimmel before getting too injured? More important was, if I stayed, what could I do to help?

A few feet from me, I saw a spear that had been dropped by a dead monster. Not sure what I would do with it, I took a few steps forward and crouched to get it.

Suddenly, a monster turned to me and wrapped his hands

around my throat. He pulled me up until I was on my tiptoes, squeezing hard, closing my airways. I fought against the dizziness while I adjusted the grip around the spear I had managed to scoop up. Bracing myself, I shoved the spear forward as fast and hard as I could.

The spear pierced his stomach, and he let go of me. I fell on my knees, and the monster fell back, writhing as he died.

Bile rose to my throat, but I didn't have time to think about it. More monsters realized I had been freed and turned to me.

I looked around for another spear, though I was sure I wouldn't be able to kill them all by myself. Just then, a strong wind blast came from the side, missing me by an inch. It took all the monsters in front of me away. They hit the wall across the room with sickening thuds; then they fell to the ground, from where they didn't rise again.

The area in front of me was mostly cleared, and I could see Cade as he swung his sword and took the head off a monster. Then he spun around, and his eyes briefly met mine. Though it had been for a second, something in his eyes told me all I needed to know.

My heart squeezed.

Cade danced in the center of the cavern, killing monsters with each one of his graceful and strong moves. I could have watched him moving like that all day long.

Something shone on the corner of my eyes. I turned and saw Delia handing a spear to Grimmel. After grabbing the spear, he pointed at me. Delia nodded once, then started after me.

Scooping up a spear in my hand, I pushed to my feet, once more trying to come up with a plan. I could try to fight

Delia, but I didn't know how to fight, much less how to wield a weapon.

Delia was close to me when I saw it. Grimmel lifted the spear above his shoulder and aimed. I gasped, looking at Cade. His back to Grimmel, he threw his hand out, blowing some monsters away. He didn't see Grimmel getting ready to kill him.

A feeling like nothing I had felt before bloomed inside me. The powerful force propelled my legs, giving them a strength and speed I could only imagine having during a zombie apocalypse.

This was worse, much worse than a zombie apocalypse.

I ran.

I just ran.

"Cade!" I screamed as Grimmel threw the spear.

Cade turned.

And I jumped into his arms, embracing him.

I felt a jolt of pain and then nothing, nothing at all, as the spear pierced my back.

I HELD Amber in my trembling arms.

"No," I whispered, not believing the sight before me. Amber had fainted the moment the spear had struck her. A spear that would have pierced through my heart and killed me instantly. She saw Grimmel throwing it and hadn't hesitated. She used herself as a shield. I heard her shallow breathing and felt the slow beating of her heart against my chest.

I raised my eyes to Grimmel. He stared at the scene like everyone else. The room had gone silent and still for a moment.

This was my opportunity. I lowered Amber on the floor, as fast and gentle as I could, and jumped. I shifted into a wolf midair and closed my jaw around Grimmel's throat before he could even blink. I ripped his throat out and turned to his lackeys.

Borak and Delia, the two monsters by his side, knelt on the ground, yelling for mercy.

They would get no mercy from me. I killed them both in

less than three seconds, then turned to the rest. They scrambled out of the cave. I got a few who had been closer, but let the rest go.

Because there was something more important than putting an end to the Tabred clan.

Amber.

I shifted back to my fae form and knelt beside her. With shaking hands, I reached for the spear in her back. I broke it as close as I could to her body, then picked her up in my arms and raced out of there.

The rest of the Tabred clan didn't attack me or try to stop me as I ran past them and out of the mountain. Holding Amber tight, I infused my veins with magic and ran. Two miles out, Kei, my six knights, and two dozen of my strongest legion awaited, hidden behind a valley. We had agreed, if I didn't come back in thirty minutes, they would invade the mountain.

Kei saw me running toward them and stepped out of his hiding spot.

"What happened?" he asked, his face ashen.

"She's dying," I said. If I stopped to think about it, I would break down. So I didn't think; I just acted. I turned to Blizzard. "I'm taking her to the healers at the palace." Kei held Amber while I jumped up on my horse. Then he gave her back to me. "Kei, Grimmel is dead, as are many of his monsters. Lead the legion into the mountain and wipe the rest out. I don't want any of them alive."

Kei hesitated but bowed his head. "Yes, my king."

I kicked Blizzard's sides, and we took off. My White Knights came with me, while Kei marched out with my legion, ready to end the Tabred clan once and for all.

At the palace, I took Amber to her bedroom. The two most capable healers arrived two minutes later. They told me to turn her on her side and keep her there while they worked on the wound.

They ripped the back of her dress, and I saw the mattress turning red with her blood. Amber whimpered with each of their tugs and touches, even though she wasn't conscious.

Lying in front of her, I held on to her shoulders, keeping her in place and watching her beautiful, sweaty face through it all, desperately trying to believe it was a simple wound and she would be okay. In a couple of hours, she would be seated in her bed, and I would yell at her for saving my life like that.

Just more proof that she was infuriatingly selfless.

The healers took the blade of the spear from her back, cleaned the wound, put some strong herbs inside it, and closed it up.

"The wound was deep, and she lost a lot of blood, but thankfully, the spear missed any vital organs," one of the healers said. "We'll keep an eye on her and avoid any infection, but now it only depends on her."

They left her bedroom, promising to be back in one hour to check on her.

I leaned in to Amber, resting my forehead on hers. "Please, my love. Please, be strong. Fight through this. Come back to me."

I didn't want to think about what came after this. All I wanted to think was that Amber would be fine. She had to be fine.

Time passed and nothing happened.

At some point, I had the guards come in and change the

mattress of Amber's bed while I took Amber to the bathroom and had Tania help me clean her up as best as we could with a soft sponge. We put a simple white nightgown on her and then laid her back on her bed.

Food was brought for Amber and for me. I didn't touch mine, but the healers had spoonfuls of soup carefully poured down Amber's throat. She coughed a few times, nearly giving me a heart attack.

The only comfort I had was the fact that she was still breathing and her heart was still beating. Otherwise, I was a wreck.

I often knelt in front of her bed and prayed. I begged Mahaera, Mahaere, and Mahaeru to let her live. *I'll do anything*, I thought. But despite all my begging and calling, the goddesses didn't come to me.

Much later, Kei came in and told me they had cleaned up the mountain as I had asked. Now I regretted being so harsh with my decision, but I was sure I would have done it again if I found myself in the same situation.

"After that, I went to check on the curse," Kei said, standing beside me. Though I paid attention to his words, my eyes were on Amber. She was sleeping in her bed, her covers pulled to her shoulders, while I watched over her from an armchair I had brought to her bedside. "I had hoped that with Grimmel dead, the curse would have broken, or that it would have at least stopped advancing." He let out a long sigh. "But it's still moving forward."

I closed my hands into fists. "So, even if Amber pulls through, I'll still have to sacrifice her to save us all."

"I'm sorry, Cade," Kei whispered.

Being sorry wasn't enough. Nothing was enough at this point.

"I have two tasks for you, Kei," I said, finally looking at him. "One, I want you to personally assemble the entire palace's staff and interview them. Make sure we don't have any more spies here. Two, gather all the scholars and officials and wise fae we have in the White City. Tell them they have four days to find a way to break the curse, one that doesn't require the sacrifice of my mate."

Kei frowned. "You want me to tell them about her sacrifice?"

I shrugged. "I don't care, as long as they find another solution."

"As you wish, my king," he said, his tone formal. He bowed his head and left the bedroom.

And I stayed with Amber for the next hour, the next day. Forever.

For two days, Amber only slept. The healers checked on her multiple times a day. No more spies had been found at the palace, the curse advanced, another village was evacuated, the scholars and officials hadn't found a solution yet. Things were getting complicated at the White City since it had many more people than it had been designed for.

And the goddesses hadn't shown their faces.

At that point, I was sure they had abandoned me. First, they had wanted to help me save the Winter Court, but now that things had gone sideways and there were no other solutions, they had disappeared.

I could only think they were afraid of my wrath, because, snow above, if Amber died *and* my land was destroyed, the world would know the wrath of the Winter Court king. The goddesses would regret not having done more when they could.

But for now, I just waited.

24

AMBER

ONCE MORE, I woke up in a different place. I was sick and tired of being knocked down and waking up somewhere else. Though I knew this place. It was my bedroom at the White Palace. Had I died and this was my version of heaven?

I rolled onto my side, and pain shot down my back. No, dreams weren't supposed to hurt this bad.

Cade was sleeping right beside me in my bed—that part was just like a delicious dream.

The fierce king of the Winter Court looked so peaceful with his gorgeous face relaxed, his long white hair a mess across the pillow, and his arms tucked under his head. Though his body—bare chest and fitted white trousers— screamed sexiness.

Was it true? Had he told the truth to Grimmel, or had he just bluffed, trying to find some kind of opening? I did feel an inexplicable pull toward him. I had been attracted to him since the first moment I laid eyes on him, and more and more each time I saw him thereafter. He had shown me a beautiful country and a warm people, even though this was the coldest place I had ever been. He fought for his land with all he had. He was kind and just.

He made me feel things I couldn't even explain.

Though he had lied to me, I now understood why. To be honest, if our roles had been reversed, I wasn't sure I wouldn't do the same thing. What was one life to save thousands? I was sure it would hurt to let go of someone you loved, but it was the only logical thing to do, even if it was the hardest.

I reached up, gritting my teeth at the soreness and pain running all over my body—who knew getting struck by a damn spear hurt so much?—and smoothed my hand over his silky hair, brushing a few strands back.

His eyes shot open, the blue in them so intense. He stared at me, as if not believing I was right there.

"Hi," I said, with a small smile.

He sucked in a sharp breath. "I'm fighting every instinct of my body to not roll over you and hug you tight." He put his hand over mine, bringing it to his cheek. "You're awake. I don't think I've ever been more grateful in my entire life." He kissed my palm, then pressed it against his cheek again. "Are you okay? Can I do anything for you? Are you hungry? Do you want me to call the healers?"

I chuckled, making my body shake slightly, and quickly stopped as new pain coursed through my back.

Cade rose on his elbows and stared at me with wide eyes. "What is it? What happened?"

"I'm fine. It's just pain," I told him.

Cade jumped from the bed, grabbed a small glass vial with maroon liquid and a spoon, and brought it to me. "Here. This should help with the pain." He poured a little of the medicine in a spoon and extended it to me. I drank it, wrinkling my nose at the foul taste. "It's bad, but it works." He dropped the vial and spoon on the nightstand and stared at me. "I can't begin to tell you how glad I am that you're alive."

"Me too." I pushed on my elbows, trying to sit up, but pain jolted across my back and I stopped. "Let me say something. I'm not sorry, because you would have died if I hadn't done that. At the same time, I'm sorry I jumped in front of you, because if I had died, I couldn't save your people."

Cade jumped in bed and over me, his body in a plank of sorts, so he was on top of me but not touching me. Even so, having him so close took my breath away. "Do you think I was worried about that?"

"I was," I admitted. I cupped his face. "That morning, I woke up alone, but I had made up my mind. I will die for your people, Cade. I wanted to tell you that right away, but I was informed you went to meet with Mahaera or one of her sisters, so I didn't want to interrupt you. Instead I went to the Moon Temple and—" I inhaled deeply. "How long has it been? How many cleansing rituals did I miss? I have to go to them now." I pushed Cade away to get up, but he didn't budge.

"Amber, listen to me."

He was so serious, so somber, I frowned. "What is it?"

"You heard what I said to Grimmel, didn't you?" His eyes searched for the answer in mine. I stilled, not even breathing. "It wasn't a lie. You're my fated mate, Amber, and that is so, so special to us fae. I can't even begin to explain it to you." My heart broke for him, for me. Cade had waited for his mate for so long, and right when he found her, this lowly human, he had to kill her to save his people. It really wasn't fair. "But I knew I loved you before that. In fact, I knew I was falling for you when you first tried to kiss me when you thought you were dreaming." I brought my hands to my face, hiding in embarrassment. With one of his big hands, he grasped both my wrists and pulled them down, so I was looking into his eyes again. "I'm serious, Amber. I love you. I love you with all my heart and soul."

"I love you too," I confessed. A new shine appeared in Cade's eyes, something so primal and sensual, I could have melted right on the spot. He leaned into me, easing his body over mine, but I threw my arms out and pushed his shoulders up, so I was still looking into his eyes when I said my next words. "And that's why I want to do this, Cade. I want to be sacrificed for your people."

He stared at me as if he hadn't heard me right. "Amber...I don't think you understand. I'll not lose you or my land. I'll find another way to have you both." He gritted his teeth. "You're *mine,* and nobody is taking you away from me ever again."

I shook my head once. "You talked to Mahaera so many times, you know there's no other way. And time is running out. Soon the curse will be here and nothing will be left to save."

Cade dropped his head on my chest. "Please, Amber, don't do this to me. I can't lose you."

I ran my hand over his hair. "You won't lose me. My body will die, but it'll restore your court. I'll live on through your land."

"No, that's not—"

"Cade," I interrupted him. A yawn followed, letting me know I was still too tired. "I don't want to argue right now. Can you just lie beside me and hold me while I sleep?"

I saw in his eyes that he wanted to keep arguing about this, but for my sake, he relented. He settled beside me and gently wrapped his arms around me. I rested my head on his shoulder, glad I could still touch him and inhale his scent. "You would think that after... how long has it been?"

"Two days," Cade said in a low voice. "You've been asleep for two days."

"So, I slept for two days, and I'm still tired."

"You almost died. That's not a little thing. Plus, the medicine you just took. It's strong against pain, but it also makes us drowsy. Even though your dose is carefully measured, I believe it's still very strong and would make you sleepy."

I hmphed. "Will you be here when I wake up?"

"Yes, my love, I will." He kissed the top of my head. "Now and forever."

I didn't think much about that "forever" in his sentence. By my calculations, this was the twelfth day since I had come to the Winter Court. In two days, I would be sacrificed in the ceremony. Our forever wouldn't last forty-eight hours, and I was even too tired to enjoy the little time I had with him.

A sliver of sorrow swirled in my chest. I didn't want to be sad about my decision. I was doing the right thing. But it still hurt having to leave Cade behind. To leave him without a mate.

I just hoped he didn't stay sad for too long.

THIS TIME, when I woke up, Cade was right there, as he promised, with breakfast and a midnight iris from the courtyard. He was gentle when helping me wash up, change clothes, and eat something. His hands lingered on me for a long time, as if he couldn't stop touching me. I wasn't complaining. In fact, I loved it. I wouldn't mind having him touching me all the time.

While Cade watched me like a hawk, I ate a little. He had his human maids make me a more human breakfast: scrambled eggs, French toast, bacon, and a strong black coffee. Though I couldn't stomach everything yet, the few bites I ate were delicious.

I loved having Cade by my side, though a heavy cloud hung over our heads. It was midmorning of my thirteenth day there. I had less than twenty-four hours to live.

"Don't you have to check on the curse or your people?" I asked. I appreciated having him with me during this time, but I didn't want him to neglect what was happening because of me.

"You're more important right now," he said, his eyes hard, his brow furrowed.

"Cade...." I rose from my chair and went to him. Though pain still radiated from my body depending on my movements, I needed to hold him. I sat on his lap, straddling him. His arms snaked around my waist, his big hands covering most of my lower back. "You have a court to run. If you forget about that because of me, I'll only feel bad about it."

"I have Kei overseeing everything," he said, his eyes locked on mine. "And I have scholars trying to find another way to save my land. It's just a matter of time before they find it."

I frowned, not sure about that. Since the goddesses had insisted there was no other way, I thought Cade was just wasting these people's time. But I didn't say anything, especially when he snaked his hand down my ass, shifting his weight under me, aligning his hips with mine.

"Cade," I whispered as my body started heating up.

"You have no idea how I wish you were better," he said, his voice husky, his eyes bright with desire. "I would be inside you right now." One of his hands rounded my thigh and slid under my nightgown, under my panties.

I sucked in a sharp breath.

A knock came from the door. Suddenly self-conscious, I jumped up from Cade's lap. Pain coursed through my back, reminding me I wasn't as well as I hoped. Gritting my teeth, I turned to the door, but before I could take one step, Cade held my wrist and said, "I'll get it."

I stayed by the table and armchairs while Cade strolled to the door and opened it.

A male fae with short white hair and wearing long white robes stood on the other side. "My king, I'm sorry to bother you."

Cade's big frame froze. "Did you find something?"

"I'm not sure, my king, but we would like to show it to you, just in case," the fae said.

Cade glanced at me.

"Go," I told him. "I'll be fine. Go see what it is."

He took four large steps to me, cupped my face, and kissed me. A fast but hard and deep kiss that left me dizzy and wanting for more. I always wanted more from him.

"I'll be right back," he whispered against my lips before marching out of the room and closing the door behind him.

I was sad to see him go but also relieved. There was something I had to do alone.

I closed my eyes and called for her. "Mahaera." As far as I knew, I could call one of them and another would show up. That was okay, as long as one of them came and talked to me. I opened my mouth, ready to call her again and beg if necessary, when I heard her voice from behind me.

"I'm here."

I turned around and faced Mahaeru, the black-haired

sister. She wore black tactical clothes that reminded me of a commander in an army. Her pose, her posture, the hardness in her dark eyes, the thin line of her lips—it all made me a little wary of her.

"I need your help," I told her.

25

CADE

THE SCHOLARS CALLED me to the library, where they had been holed up for the last two days, going over all the books and knowledge, not only of Winter Court but also all of Wyth.

Deep down, I knew they wouldn't find anything. Mahaera had told me there was no other solution. And yet, I hoped. I had to hope, because I couldn't imagine holding the ceremony tomorrow.

But as I arrived at the library and went through the scholars' notes, I realized that all they had were theories—really bad ones.

I smacked a notebook on the table. "Does anyone have anything concrete? That you know will work, no matter what? That we can put into practice right now?"

All the scholars lowered their heads.

"I'm sorry, my king," one of them said in a cowering voice.

A wave of rage swept through me. They had me called away from Amber for this?

"Keep trying!" I barked. "You've got twelve hours to find a real, concrete way of stopping the curse."

With that, I exited the library before I broke something. On the way back to Amber's bedroom, I ran into Kei, who had stopped by to take a quick shower before going back to the White City to do my job. I felt bad for all he had to do for me these past few days. I would compensate him for all of that later.

"I'm on my way to start evacuating another village," Kei said, his voice somber. "This is the last village before the White City, Cade. We should start thinking about evacuating the people here too."

I rubbed my fingertips on my temple, feeling a headache coming. "Not yet, Kei. Not yet. I can't think about that just yet."

"I understand," Kei said. "We can wait another two days."

Two days. As if he didn't know what was scheduled for tomorrow morning. My heart tugged as despair enveloped me. There wasn't enough time. I had to do something.

"You're doing a great job, Kei," I told him half-heartedly. "Keep it up for now, please."

"Will do." Kei bowed his head and walked toward the back of the palace, where he would probably get his horse and gallop to the next village to be evacuated.

I was losing my frosting mind.

I couldn't imagine evacuating the White City and the White Palace, the hearts of the Winter Court, and yet, what other freezing choice did I have? I wasn't going to kill Amber; I had already decided that.

But if I didn't sacrifice her, then my city would be lost.

This was an impossible situation. I couldn't choose between my mate and my court. I just couldn't.

Decided, I went to my study and grabbed the medallion from the drawer under my desk. Perhaps it wasn't the best solution, but it was the only one I had right then. I tucked the medallion in the pocket of my cloak and raced back to Amber's bedroom.

The guards stepped to the side when they saw me and allowed me to go in.

I frowned as I looked around her bedroom. "Amber?" I called out. No answer. My heart pounded as I checked the closet and the bathroom. "Amber?" My voice rose in confusion and despair. "Amber!" I went back to the door, opened it, and asked the guards. "Did Amber leave?"

Niossal frowned. "No, my king. You were the only one in and out of this room today."

"She isn't here," I muttered, the blood in my veins rushing in my ears.

"What? How?" Niossal stared inside.

"I know where she is."

I turned back to the room and found Mahaeru standing beside the bed. I clenched my fists. "What did you do to her?"

"Nothing she didn't want me to do," the goddess said.

"What does that mean?"

"Amber asked me to take her until the ceremony tomorrow," Mahaeru said. "We'll perform it at the main road, right in front of the curse."

My magic crackled in my fingers. "Snow above, I will strike you if you don't return Amber to me right now!"

"Go ahead, strike me." Mahaeru lifted her chin and puffed her chest, serving as a big target for me. "You'll only be dooming your land further."

I gritted my teeth, wanting—needing to do something. But what? I exhaled and let go of my magic. "Mahaeru, please, don't do this to me. There has to be another way."

"I'm sorry, Cadewyn. To save the Winter Court, a human

life has to end in a sacrifice." She paused. "Don't worry. I'll make sure Amber doesn't feel any pain."

"Please," I said, my voice breaking.

"I expect to see you there tomorrow."

Then she disappeared.

And I let out a scream that shook the walls of the palace.

***

I DIDN'T SLEEP. I didn't eat. I didn't stop pacing around my study, demanding answers. From the scholars and from the goddesses—though the goddesses ignored all my calls.

None of the answers satisfied me. The scholars couldn't find a way to break the curse, and in a few hours, it would take another village and come for the White City next.

Everything was crumbling at my feet, and there was nothing I could do. Nothing. Right then, I was a king without the power to save my people, to save my mate.

I never felt so desperate and helpless in my entire life.

When it was time to go, Kei came for me. "Are you okay?" he asked. I glared at him. "Stupid question." I started walking, but he blocked the door. "Are you sure you want to come? Perhaps witnessing the ceremony will be too hard."

I had thought about it, but.... "I can't not come."

Kei stared at me for a moment. Then he nodded and stepped to the side. He and the White Knights rode with me through the main road out of the White City until it met with the advancing curse in the south.

My heart sank at the view before me. Beyond the curse, everything was black and dead. But my heart sank even more when I saw the little white wood dais set up a few yards from the curse, with a long table on top.

The priestesses of the Moon Temple were already around the dais, but there was no sign of Mahaeru, or one of her versions, and Amber.

"Where are they?" I asked the priestesses.

One priestess turned to me and opened her mouth to answer. Instead, her eyes widened and she pointed behind me.

I whirled around and saw Amber standing beside Mahaeru on the other side of the dais.

Amber's eyes locked on mine, and my breath caught. She looked divine in a simple, long white dress and jacket with her black hair tied in a tight braid.

She offered me a small smile, and a pain stabbed me deep in my core. Snow above, this wasn't happening. I went to her, wrapped my arms around her, and held her tight against me.

"Please don't do this," I whispered in her ear.

She rose on her tiptoes and brought her lips to mine. She started the gentle kiss, but I took control, deepening it, molding my mouth to hers, moving in a frantic rhythm, tasting her, savoring her, marking her.

She was mine. Mine.

And I was about to lose her.

Slowly, Amber pulled back. I held on to her, but she broke the kiss and looked into my eyes. "I've got to do this, Cade. There's a reason why I was chosen, why I was called pure-hearted and selfless. This is me being selfless."

I locked my arms around her. "I can't let you do this."

"Please, Cade, don't make this more difficult," she said, her voice low. "Just remember I love you. I'll always love you." She pressed her lips to mine again, then stepped back, pushing against my arms.

I didn't want to let her go. I couldn't.

"Cadewyn, if you don't comply with this ceremony of your own will, I'll make you," Mahaeru said, her voice harsh. "And I promise you, you'll regret it."

"Please, Cade," Amber whispered. "She told me that if you don't behave, she'll take you away from here. I know this might be hard, but I really would like you here for me."

Something burned behind my eyes. Defeated, I dropped my arms.

Amber showed me that soft smile again before climbing the dais with Mahaeru.

I watched, my eyes round. No, no, no. I wouldn't let her do this. My mate couldn't be killed. This was insane.

With a growl, I advanced toward the dais.

And met an invisible wall that pushed me back several feet. "What the frost?"

"It's for your own good, Cade," Mahaeru warned. "And stay quiet, or I'll do something about your voice too."

Kei grabbed my shoulders and pulled me back a few steps. Suddenly, I didn't have the strength to fight back, not when Mahaeru helped Amber to the table, where my mate lay down and awaited her fate.

Mahaeru and the priestesses started chanting in their own language, and I felt their power rising from the ground. Meanwhile, the curse advanced, just a foot from the dais.

A moment later, a dagger appeared in Mahaeru's hand. She lifted the weapon high.

My legs gave out, and I fell on my knees.

Mahaeru plunged the dagger into Amber's chest.

Her dark red blood slipped down from the table to a hole on the dais, falling on the ground just as the curse advanced some more. The blood touched the curse.

A shudder seemed to shake the entire land.

There was a long pause—no one breathed, no one blinked. The Winter Court seemed frozen. Then, slowly, the curse started retreating.

"It worked!" Kei cried.

It had worked at the expense of Amber's life.

I curled into myself, roaring and punching the ground below me, and cried.

I OPENED my eyes and stared at the blue skies. Was this heaven? Did I deserve to go to heaven? I wasn't that perfect and sinless....

"Are you okay?"

I whipped my head to the side and found Mahaera standing beside me. I frowned. "Am I dead? What are you doing here?"

"I'll explain everything. Just tell me what you're feeling first." She offered me her hand.

I took her hand, and she helped me sit up. My dress, once white, was now drenched in red. My blood. I had died, hadn't I?

I frowned, trying to understand what was going on. "I feel a tingling under my skin." I blinked, looking at the horizon covered in snow. "The colors, even the white of the snow, are much sharper." I glanced around and froze when I saw the curse slowly retreating. "It worked?"

Mahaera nodded. "It did. What else are you feeling?"

I stared at the blackened land for a second more, then

focused on the goddess's question. "My hearing...." I gasped, turning to glance at Cade. He was kneeling a few feet from the dais, his head down, and crying softly. I could hear him sniffing and muttering curses at Mahaeru and Grimmel under his breath. "I can hear much more than before."

"This too." Mahaera guided my hand to my ear.

I traced it and gasped again. It was pointed, just like a fae's. "What's going on?" I asked, my voice pitching high in confusion.

At that, Cade heard me. With wide eyes, he stood and walked closer. "Amber...?"

Mahaera smiled at me. "The sacrifice demanded a human life. You gave your human life to save the Winter Court."

I frowned. "I don't understand."

"You are pure-hearted and selfless," Mahaera said. "I knew the land, which is the most powerful being of all the fae realm, would recognize your worth. So I prepared you for this." She gestured to the new me. "The cleansing ritual wasn't necessary for this ceremony, but it was necessary if the land decided to save you somehow."

"You saved me," I whispered in awe.

Mahaera shrugged. "It was a joint effort."

My eyes filled with tears. "Thank you."

"Now you can enjoy a long fae life." She turned and beckoned Cade forward. He hesitated, testing if the invisible wall was still up, but once he was sure it wasn't, he raced to me. He wound his arms around me and pulled me to him. "With your mate."

Cade turned his head to Mahaera. "Thank you, Mahaera. I don't know how to repay you."

"I didn't do it for you, Cadewyn," Mahaera said. "I did it for the balance of Wyth." She smiled at me. "I hope you continue to be pure-hearted and selfless, even in your fae life."

She bowed her head at me. I blinked, and she was gone.

Holding me tight, Cade buried his head in my shoulder. "I thought I lost you." He pulled back to look at me, one of his hands smoothing down my head and braid. "You're mine now, as you were meant to be, and I'm never letting you go."

For a moment, my brows slanted down. Before, when I thought they just needed me for a simple ceremony, all I wanted was to go back to the human world, even though I didn't have anything waiting for me there. Didn't I want that now? What would I go back to? No job, no money, a drunken roommate, a shitty apartment. What I could do was go back to tell Kimberly I was leaving, pick up some of my things that were dear to me, and come back here to be with Cade.

Never before had I felt surer of something. I loved Cade with all my heart, and he was my home, wherever that was.

With a small smile, I snaked my arms around his shoulders. "I like that."

Mahaera smiled at us. "It's done. Congratulations."

I held Amber's hand and tugged her closer to me. My will was to crash into her and kiss her until she was breathless, but I shouldn't do it in front of so many guests. I pressed my lips to hers, lingering for a moment, sending a promise of what was to come later. Still holding her hand, I turned to our guests. Amber did the same, clearly still not used to the spotlight. We waved and bowed our heads to our guests, who clapped enthusiastically.

I glanced at Amber. She was simply radiant in an intricate silver dress and crystal drops woven among her long, dark hair. What I felt for her...there were no words to describe it. She was my lover, my mate, my best friend, and now my wife.

It had been six months since she sacrificed her human life for my court. The curse had retreated completely, but the destruction it had left behind hadn't been undone. We had been working tirelessly to rebuild every village, every road, every snowcapped garden that had been destroyed. We had made much progress, but there was still a lot of work ahead of us.

I loved having Amber by my side, helping our people, guiding them, and comforting them during the tumultuous time we faced. And the people loved her. They were already charmed by her when she was human, but they fell completely in love with her once they learned she laid her own life down for them. For me. Every day, I prayed to Mahaera, Mahaere, Mahaeru, and the land, thanking them for their benevolence. I had considered myself a fair king so far, but now I would be even more just and care for my people even better, all to honor what they had done for Amber and me.

With the curse and the attempts on Amber's life, I was still wary of the Tywyll Forest, though. Kei had told me he had cleaned up the mountain as I had asked, and I believed him, but it didn't mean a few didn't get away somehow. But more than just the Tabred clan, what I wanted was to keep every monster from the Tywyll Forest away, so I joined forces with Amber, Mahaeru, and Tenen, the king of the Day Court, to create a magical barrier that would stop anyone from the Tywyll Forest who tried to infiltrate our lands. We had sealed off that part of the continent for good.

During the sealing spell, Amber had surprised me. She had been practicing her magic with appointed instructors, and sometimes with Mahaera when the goddess felt like stopping by, but I hadn't known just how powerful she was until she insisted she help with the spell. Her magic was almost as strong as mine.

Every day, she surprised me. Every day, I was more enamored with her.

I brought her hand to my lips and kissed her knuckles. Her cheeks gained a red tint.

I guided her through the set-up aisle inside the Moon Temple, amidst the guests, along the stone path outside, and into the ballroom of the White Palace, where we received all our guests to celebrate our union with us.

The band played harmonious music, the drinks were already being served, and soon delicious food would be brought out. Tonight would be a night to remember forever.

I introduced Amber to so many royal and higher fae, her mind was probably reeling by the end of the night.

"Amber, this is Natsia, the queen of the Summer Court," I said, gesturing to the tall female fae with smooth, dark skin and wise hazel eyes.

"It's a pleasure to meet the savior of the Winter Court," Natsia said, smiling at Amber.

Amber's cheeks gained a pink tint. "The pleasure is mine,"

"And this is Prince Varian, her son." I showed her to the male fae by the queen's side. He was just a few years younger than me. When we were children, we used to play together during events, mostly a teasing fight while we showed off our opposite powers.

"Enchanted," he said with a lopsided grin.

"Likewise," Amber replied.

"King Cadewyn, I hate to bring up such a dreadful topic during a gleeful ceremony, but I need to tell you something," Natsia said, taking one small step closer to us. "My sources tell me King Vasant is gathering his forces and training them vigorously."

"As if he's preparing them for war," Varian added.

I frowned. Even though they were from different courts,

Vasant was Natsia's cousin, as his mother was a princess of the Summer Court, sister to Natsia's father. Vasant's mother married his father right before he was crowned king of the Spring Court long ago. Once upon a time, the Summer and the Spring Courts had been strong allies, the strongest when together. But then the civil war happened at the Spring Court, and the Summer Court broke that alliance.

"If that's true, then it means Vasant has a plan," I mused. And knowing Vasant and his ruthless ways, it couldn't be anything good. "Why don't we enjoy the party for tonight, and before your departure tomorrow, we have a meeting about that?"

Natsia smiled. "Splendid."

After meeting the queen and prince of the Summer Court, I introduced Amber to the famous twins of the Night Court, Prince Nox and Princess Amaya.

Princess Amaya smiled at Amber. "You're more beautiful than the rumors."

Prince Nox kissed Amber's hand. "If you ever get tired of this old man, you know where to find me." He winked at her. Amber's mouth dropped, but I just chuckled, knowing Nox was teasing her.

From there, I introduced her to Altan and Zora, the king and queen from the Dawn Court. And she already knew Tenen, the king of the Day Court, but she met Hemera, his wife and queen.

Before the ceremony, I told Amber some of the courts weren't coming to our wedding. First, we hadn't invited Vasant, because after what he did to Amber, he wasn't welcome here anymore, not even for political matters. The Dusk Court was usually very quiet and never participated in any special events with other courts, though they had sent a beautiful jewel as a gift. And the Autumn Court had sent a short letter saying they were sorry but would have to miss the wedding.

After going around the room and greeting everyone, Amber and I danced for hours, ate too much, drank a little, laughed, smiled, and kissed. I didn't think I had ever been happier. I still had work to do with my court to make it prosperous and beautiful again, but with Amber by my side, I was sure it would be even better than before.

I spun her under my arm and pulled her to me again. A little dizzy with her drink, she yelped at the impact and splayed her hands over my shoulders. She held on to me, grazing my skin through the fabric of my shirt with her long nails, sending a wave of heat through my entire body.

I leaned into her and whispered in her ear, "How about we get out of here?"

She pulled back and looked into my eyes. "That's a great idea."

I knotted my hands in hers and whisked her from the ballroom. I didn't bother saying goodbye to anyone, since most had come from far away and would spend the night in the palace. Tomorrow we would have a big lunch at one of the winter rooms, where we could properly bid farewell to our guests.

Amber and I raced up the stairs, ignoring the White Knights following us, and went into my—*our*—chambers.

I closed the doors behind us and stared at the beautiful female fae in front of me, desire igniting my core.

My mate, my lover, my wife.

Mine.

Only mine.

I TURNED to Cade as he stepped back from the locked door, giving him a come-hither look. The shine in his light-blue eyes darkened as he advanced on me, hunger written all over his face.

Hunger for me.

My stomach tightened as he lunged at me, winding his arms around my body and claiming my mouth. Kissing me, teasing me with his tongue, Cade guided me back, across the sitting area, past the archway, and into our bedroom. He pushed me against the wall beside the long windows, pressing his body against mine. Even through this thick dress, I felt his massive hard-on.

And it was all for me.

His hands found the clasps of the dress, and he tugged at them, practically ripping it open. As the dress slipped down my body, Cade broke the kiss and took off his shirt and pants. After I stepped out of the dress, he gently kicked it aside so it was out of the way. Then he stepped back into me, but instead of kissing me as I was expecting, he turned me around. I gasped as he splayed my hands on the wall and pressed his hot chest to my back, his cock poised at my ass.

He pushed my hair to the side and inhaled deeply.

I moaned as he closed his hands around my breasts and played with my nipples, rolling his fingers over the hardened buds and pinching gently. Letting out moans I couldn't control, I squirmed, rubbing my ass onto his hard-on.

He slid one of his hands down my stomach to my pussy. I gasped when he grazed his fingers across my inner thighs, teasing me, making me hotter and more desperate. Then he slipped two fingers inside me. I let out a hiss and bucked against his hand. Holy shit, his hand was amazing.

He leaned his head on my shoulder, first placing a soft kiss on my skin, then biting it gently, all the while devouring me with his fingers.

"Cade," I whispered, far too gone.

My core tightened around his fingers. I knew he could feel that. I was close. Thankfully, he slid his other hand down and rubbed my clit with his thumb.

That was all it took. I leaned back on him as I came, trembling against him.

Cade kept teasing me, rubbing his cock on my pussy. He pressed his chest on my back and put his mouth on my ear. "What do you want?"

I moaned. "You, holy shit. Just take me."

A growl ripped from his chest, and in one powerful stroke, he filled me up, going oh so deep. "You're so frosting wet," he said, shuddering. He bit my shoulder again. "You feel so good."

"Cade," I hissed, pushing my ass back toward him. "Shut up and just do me."

Clasping my waist, Cade moved. He pulled his cock all

the way out and pushed in, hard and deep. I gasped but couldn't help myself. "More," I panted. "Give me more."

With another growl, Cade obliged. He pumped into me with all he had.

Eyes half closed, I threw my head back, surrendering to the pleasure. Cade trailed his lips along my neck, sending shivers of pure sensation down my spine. He nipped at my earlobe and glided his hands from my waist to my breasts. He pinched the hard nipples, and I let out a cry.

Suddenly, Cade pulled out of me, and in one swift move, picked me up in his arms. I yelped but didn't complain as he carried me to our bed.

He paused for a moment, watching me spread myself over the sheets, biting my lower lip, knowing he was feeling as aroused as I was.

Cade crawled over me, and I grazed my long nails over his chest and his stomach, loving the feel of the many muscles he sported. The man was a freaking god, at least to me.

And he was all mine.

I wrapped my hand around his cock, and he bucked.

"Hm, so hard, so thick."

He dropped his head, resting his forehead on mine. "It's all because of you."

I smiled and pumped my hand over his length once, twice, three times. He hissed and closed his eyes. I loved when he lost control and surrendered to the feelings. Then, I slipped my other hand around his hip and tugged him closer. Still holding his cock, I guided it into me.

"Snow above," he whispered, his tone husky.

I wound my legs around his waist, lifting my hips and pulling him even deeper. He tensed, visibly trying to hold on for longer. I smiled and sank my nails in his back as he thrust into me with long, deep strokes. Then I tensed. Holy shit, I was almost there again.

Cade knew it too, because he pushed even harder into me, stealing little moans from my throat. Then I stilled for a moment and came around him. Cade kept pumping into me a few more times, not easing my climax, until he was also a goner. He gritted his teeth and fell over me, his body trembling along with mine.

I kept my arms and legs around him for a long time, appreciating this moment.

Then Cade lifted his head and watched me. "Ready for eternity with me?"

I smiled at him. "Hell yes."

Cade chuckled. He had been smiling and laughing more and more, and I just loved seeing him so happy. He smoothed his hand over my head. "I love you, Queen Amber. With all my heart and soul."

"I love you more, King Cadewyn."

He lowered his mouth to mine and kissed me—a long, soft kiss full of promises and possibilities.

I was still getting used to being a fae. I still had a lot to learn and do, but there was one thing I knew wouldn't ever change, even in my now super-long life: my love for Cade and his love for me.

CONTINUE READING about our sexy fae and their beloved mates with *Spring Warrior*, the second book in The Wyth Courts series! Get it now!

THANK YOU

THANK you for reading *Winter King*!

Reviews are very important for authors. If you liked my book, please consider leaving a review on your favorite online retailer and/or on goodreads, please!

GET BOOK 2 NOW: *Spring Warrior*

DON'T FORGET to sign up for my Newsletter to find out about new releases, cover reveals, giveaways, and more!

If you want to see exclusive teasers, help me decide on covers, read excerpts, talk about books, etc, join my reader group on Facebook: Juliana's Club!

ABOUT THE AUTHOR

While USA Today Bestselling Author Juliana Haygert dreams of being Wonder Woman, Buffy, or a blood elf shadow priest, she settles for the less exciting—but equally gratifying—life as a wife, a mother, and an author. She resides in North Carolina and spends her days writing about kick-ass heroines and the heroes who drive them crazy.

Subscribe to her mailing list to receive emails of announcement, events, and other fun stuff related to her writing and her books: www.bit.ly/JuHNL

For more information:
www.julianahaygert.com

facebook.com/julianahaygert

twitter.com/juliana_haygert

instagram.com/juliana.haygert

goodreads.com/juliana_haygert

pinterest.com/julianahaygert

bookbub.com/authors/juliana-haygert

ALSO BY JULIANA HAYGERT

To find links and more info, go to:

www.julianahaygert.com/books/

Shorts

Into the Darkest Fire

Tested

Rite World: Blackthorn Hunters Academy

The Demon Kiss (Book 1)

The Hunter Secret (Book 2)

The Soul Bond (Book 3)

The Shadow Trials (Book 4)

The Infernal Curse (Book 5)

Rite World

The Vampire Heir (Book 1)

The Witch Queen (Book 2)

The Immortal Vow (Book 3)

The Warlock Lord (Book 4)

The Wolf Consort (Book 5)

The Crystal Rose (Book 6)

The Wolf Forsaken (Book 7)

The Fae Bound (Book 8)

The Blood Pact (Book 9)

The Wyth Courts

Winter King (Book 1)

Spring Warrior (Book 2)

Summer Prince (Book 3)

The Fire Heart Chronicles

Heart Seeker (Book 1)

Flame Caster (Book 2)

Sorrow Bringer (Book 3)

Earth Shaker (Novella)

Soul Wanderer (Book 4)

Fate Summoner (Book 5)

War Maiden (Book 6)

The Everlast Series

Destiny Gift (Book 1)

Soul Oath (Book 2)

Cup of Life (Book 3)

Everlasting Circle (Book 4)

Willow Harbor Series

Hunter's Revenge (Book 3)

Siren's Song (Book 5)

Breaking Series

Breaking Free (Book 1)

Breaking Away (Book 2)

Breaking Through (Book 3)

Breaking Down (Book 4)

Standalones

Daughter of Darkness